"Welcome to the new and improved Nick's. What would you like this evening?" the deep voice asked her, his warm breath close to her neck.

The hairs on Morgan's arms rose, and she could feel the beads of perspiration forming on her brow. She opened her mouth to speak, but quickly shut her mouth as she took in the large form standing over her. His muscular arms strained against the fabric of his black and white striped jersey, which proudly displayed the name of the bar across his wide chest. She smiled brightly as she looked up into Jarrod's light eyes.

"Hey, beautiful." Jarrod smiled as he looked down at Morgan. "I had wondered if you'd heard about the reopening. How've you been?"

Morgan could feel the silly grin on her face as she fought to remain seated, when what she wanted to do was to jump into the arms of this six foot, muscular 250 pound, chocolate brother whose smile melted her insides and whose intense eyes arrested her good sense. *Now, why couldn't I meet a man like Jarrod.*

CUPID

BARBARA KEATON

Genesis Press, Inc.

Indigo

An imprint of Genesis Press, Inc.
Publishing Company

Genesis Press, Inc.
P.O. Box 101
Columbus, MS 39703

ISBN: 1-58571-174-8
Manufactured in the United States of America

First Edition

Visit us at www.genesis-press.com
or call at 1-888-Indigo-1

DEDICATION

This book is dedicated to my mother, Aurelia Keaton. Mom, dreams aren't always measurable, but blessings are insurmountable. Thank you for being a blessing to me.

ACKNOWLEDGMENTS

As always, I thank my Lord, and Jesus Christ from whom all my blessings flow. In addition, many thanks to my family and friends for their constant and unending support! I love y'all! And to CR—I'm holding out for a hero!

CHAPTER 1

"If you ever put your hands on me again," Morgan sneered, her nose inches from his face, "I swear you will draw back a nub." She straightened, and then smiled demurely, her head cocked to the left. She tossed the fork onto the table. Her threat worked, and she watched Thomas, her first, and she wanted to swear her last, blind date, sit back in his chair. His face became a twisted mass of confusion and embarrassment.

Morgan sighed and shook her head as he tossed back his seventh drink. Her eyebrows raised high over her eyes when Thomas stood quickly. His eyes rolled into the back of his head just before all six foot-four of him fell to the floor. The table and a few chairs went with him. Morgan's first instinct was to leave him there, it would serve him right she thought. Instead, she brushed her shoulder-length, sun-kissed brown twists from her face and marched over to the greeter he had shamelessly flirted with when she first arrived. She instructed the greeter to call Thomas a cab.

The patrons in the restaurant stared. A few laughed out loud as Thomas lay sprawled out on the restaurant floor. Morgan took one look at him, the all-important Thomas Van Norton, Esquire, stone cold drunk, passed out on the crumb-filled restaurant floor. She tried to stifle the giggle that began in the pit of her abdomen. But, the more she tried, the harder it became, until she gave up and began to laugh aloud.

Morgan wiped the tears of laughter from her eyes as she walked back to where he lay. She squatted next to him and patted him lightly across his slim cheeks in an attempt to bring him around to some semblance of semi-consciousness. He stirred. She patted him again, this time a little harder. Thomas' eyes fluttered, and he groaned as his long arms reached toward her.

"Thomas," Morgan leaned closer and whispered into his ear. "Get up." On cue, Thomas began to rise on wobbly legs. Morgan assisted him to his feet, and could not help but snicker as she brushed food and dirt off his expensive-looking navy blue suit. She asked their waiter for the bill. Thomas leaned heavily on her five-foot-five frame as she struggled to open her purse. She pulled several bills from her purse, handed them to the waiter, then took Thomas by his hand and led him outside. She sat him on the steps of the restaurant, leaned Thomas on the iron banister and walked away.

She turned once more and began to laugh again. Lips pursed, she said a silent prayer. She knew that God always protected babies and fools. And Thomas was definitely a fool!

A smile tipped her lips as she inhaled deeply and looked up into the midnight sky. She buttoned her nutmeg colored leather coat and placed her small hands into matching leather driving gloves. The bright stars overhead twinkled as they surrounded the pale blue autumn half moon. She looked at her watch. The night was still young, and after this blind date, she didn't particularly want to head home, especially on a Friday night.

She retrieved her cell phone from her purse and dialed Yavette. After the extension rang four times, she heard the pause indicating she would have to leave her cousin a voice mail message.

"Girl!" Morgan squealed into the receiver. "You owe me one. Big time!" She looked over her shoulder to where she had left Thomas and began to laugh again. Thomas had curled up in a fetal position at the foot of the restaurant steps. "Call me when you get a chance. Bye." She disconnected the call and headed to her car. Her mind, body and spirit wouldn't allow her to go home and dwell on the events of the night.

She thought of how Yavette had talked her into going on a series of blind dates, beginning with one of Yavette's co-workers. She shook her head as she slid behind the seat of her emerald green Jaguar, then fished around in the glove compartment for the flier announcing the grand re-opening of Nick's Sports Bar & Grille someone had left on the windshield of her car. She'd glanced at it, then tossed it into the glove compartment. *Wow.* She hadn't been to Nick's in ages. She missed her old haunt, her Friday night getaway where, as the song from Cheers stated, "everybody knows your name." She smiled and looked at the flier. The image flooded her mind instantly, and she wondered if he was still there—the man with the warm eyes, tight physique and sexy dimples—her favorite bartender. Jarrod had become one of the main reasons Morgan frequented Nick's—his searing good looks made even hotter with the conversations she had had with him. Admittedly, she liked Jarrod. And had found him on more than one occasion tipping around in her fantasies, his full lips close to hers, her body held tight against his large chest. Now, if she could get a hook-up with Jarrod.

No, Morgan sighed, he hadn't seemed interested in her. Yes, he had always listened to her and was quick with uplifting words, but that was the extent of it. He'd never inquired about her outside of the confines of the bar. She thought of the last time she had been inside of Nick's, two weeks before they closed for renovations. She had sat at the bar and watched as Jarrod went about tending bar, fixing drinks and flashing his kilowatt smile. As she watched him pour her drink in the jewel-encrusted glass with her name written in gold script lettering that he had ordered for her, she was filled with an odd sense of sadness. At the end of the night, Jarrod had walked her to her car. As they stood there, she watched him fidget. His foot played along the cracks in the concrete. She knew he had something to say, and when she quizzed him, he said it was nothing, gave her a quick peck on her cheek, opened her car door for her, then shut it and walked off. That was the last time Morgan had seen Jarrod, over six months ago.

"Just what the doctor ordered," Morgan joked to herself. "Besides, eight o'clock is way too early to head home."

As she headed to Nick's, she thought of how she, Morgan Deneen Paige, proud owner and president of Paige Public Relations, had gotten into the situation of Yavette hooking her with blind dates in the first place. It was her big mouth several months ago, when she and Yavette had talked about Morgan's dating, or lack thereof. Next thing she knew, Yavette was arranging blind dates.

"He's fine, girl," Yavette had said a few weeks earlier as she sat across from her during lunch. "And he said he's looking for a serious relationship—isn't looking to play games. To top it off, he's a partner at the firm, so he's financially secure."

Morgan glanced at the cousin who was barely five months her junior and who had been more like a sister to her. She had tried to listen intently as Yavette went on describing her first blind date, Thomas Van Norton, who worked at the same law firm Yavette did. Morgan wanted to kick her own butt for even mentioning to Yavette that she had surfed the Internet personals, which she surmised had gotten Yavette into wanting to match her with someone. What she hadn't told Yavette was that she had already agreed to meet one of the men she had met. Instead, Morgan had told Yavette that the men she had met online didn't interest her past a chat room.

"You're both looking for a mate. You're both professionals. Both single, though he's never been married, and neither of you have any children. I say you two should be perfect for each other. Let me fix you up," Yavette had said as she stabbed at the shrimp salad the waiter had placed in front of her. After nearly another thirty minutes of bantering, Morgan reluctantly agreed.

On the night of the date, Morgan stood in her favorite restaurant and glanced at her wristwatch several times as she tapped her boot-clad heel against the wood floor. Her eyes took in several male faces while her mind replayed the description Yavette had given her. She said he was tall and handsome. Period. Morgan had begged for a more detailed description, but Yavette had shrugged her shoulders and stated, "You'll see."

Morgan looked at her watch again. Late. *This brother is twenty minutes late*, Morgan had said to herself as she looked at her watch for the umpteenth time. As she lifted her head, she spied a tall brother, at least six-foot=four, his skin the color of graham crackers. She watched as he approached and instinctively knew that Thomas Van Norton had arrived. Already he had amassed a strike—strike one was his late arrival. And Yavette had to be color blind, Morgan thought as she watched Thomas step into the restaurant, because this man was not brown skinned or chocolate chip like Jarrod. Morgan almost gasped aloud as she wondered where that thought came from.

As he approached, Morgan thought about how Yavette had said that Thomas was at the top of his game and searching for a secure woman to stand by his side. Morgan had huffed at that statement. A secure man begets a secure woman, and most of the men she had met professionally were far from secure. Even her ex-husband, Michael. She shook loose the thoughts that threatened to invade her. Not right now. Now was not the time to go back down that Memory Lane.

When Thomas opened the door to the restaurant, she noted that his narrow nose was raised a bit high and his lips pursed, as if the air of the restaurant offended all his senses. She smirked. From the looks of it, Thomas, the lawyer and partner of a prestigious law firm, thought he was all that, a family-sized bag of chips and a six-pack of Pepsi. She wondered what made Yavette think they would get along. Morgan was earthier, like her father, and Thomas appeared worldlier—like the world revolved around him. Maybe this Thomas person hadn't been straight with Yavette. Morgan shrugged and thought she wasn't being fair and decided to at least give him the benefit of the doubt. Then she paused. She watched him closely as he stepped past her, didn't even look her way, approached the greeter, and then leaned his lanky frame on the short counter. Morgan smirked as he glared at the greeter's full bust line, which begged for a much larger blouse.

Strike two! Morgan liked her men with meat on their bones. Thomas' frame was slight. And she wasn't too keen on watching him size up the greeter as if she were a smothered pork chop on the menu.

Enough. Morgan blew out through clenched teeth. *Forget the benefit. Lets get this over with.*

"Thomas?" Morgan stepped forward as she called out his name.

"The one and only. And you are?" His small gray eyes roved from the top of her head to her boot-clad feet.

Morgan gritted her teeth into a smile. She wanted to walk right out, but her stomach protested. She'd eaten very little that day, knowing that she would make up for it by feasting on the mustard catfish with a side of mean greens and a cornbread muffin.

"I'm Morgan."

"Oh." His eyes raked over her once more. "A pleasure, I'm sure." He bent at the waist and took her hand in his, placing a wet kiss on the back of her hand. An overwhelming urge to snatch her hand from him and slap him across his round head crept down Morgan's arm. Instead, she indulged him as she partook in the grandiose gesture by curtsying slightly.

How trite, she thought as he straightened. She watched as he scanned the small restaurant, his mouth again pursed in a pout. She detected he wasn't exactly pleased with her choice. *Umm, strike three! This brother done struck out!* Dixie Kitchen and Bait Shop restaurant was one of Morgan's top 10 favorite restaurants.

"Shall we?" He took her by the elbow and waited as the greeter came around from the counter and escorted them to their seats. Morgan watched as Thomas' eyes seemed glued to the woman's full backside.

Damn! This brother is now so far out of the ballpark that he's sitting on the bus stop bench at the corner of Federal and 35th Street. At this point, Morgan no longer wanted to walk out—she wanted to run. This was definitely not for her. She couldn't wait to speak with Yavette to see what was on her mind!

Once seated, Morgan got a good look at her date. His cleanly shaven face sported chiseled features and a slightly narrowed nose. His thin lips and square chin jutted out from his face and made him look more like a model, somewhat feminine. The one thing in his favor was his suit. Morgan figured the suit was tailor made, the way the jacket fit his slender shoulders, perfectly tapered, and was complimented with a stark white shirt and maroon tie, ending with a pair of freshly polished, navy, cap-toe shoes. She had to admit, he was impeccably groomed, and she liked that in a man, but there was something about his smile—

the way his thin lips spread across his too white teeth. *Cosmetic,* she thought. Still, his smile seemed to be more of a leer.

"Umph," he said.

"Did you say something?" Morgan watched his eyes turn a smoky gray as they fixed themselves on the form of her top. His eyes held a lascivious glint to them.

"Sister, did I tell you that you are more beautiful than Yavette described? That picture she showed me of the two of you does you no justice." He leaned over the table and leered at her. Morgan reeled back, and her shoulders pressed against her chair. She knew the picture he was talking about. It was the one she and Yavette had taken in Puerto Rico nearly two years earlier. Both of them had on two-piece tankinis and had turned their backsides to the camera. She shook her head. To add to it, the picture reminded her of Michael, and their divorce, which had become final a week before the picture was taken. When Morgan thought about it, they hadn't parted on bad terms. To put it simply, they had just fallen out of love with each other. The thought of that statement always made her sullen. She wondered how at one time two people so in love could just fall out of it.

Thomas flicked his business card from the inside breast pocket of his suit and handed it to the greeter as she passed their table.

"If you ever *need* a lawyer."

Morgan twisted her mouth. The emphasis he had had placed on "need" wasn't lost on her.

As they scanned the menu, Thomas continually glared at the space between the top of the table and Morgan's neck. Not once did he look into her misty brown eyes. Instead, he seemed to prefer to stare at the form her breasts made against the turtleneck she wore. She folded her arms across her chest, which only intensified his leer. She looked down at her attire. She was dressed in a camel-colored turtleneck, a mocha brown wool blazer and camel-colored, wool slacks. Nothing to glare at. Still, the look in his eyes made her think he could see past her bra and panties down to her bare flesh.

"So, tell me about yourself," Thomas whispered. Morgan sniffed. *Alcohol. The brother's been drinking already.* "I hear you own your own business. Yavette says you are quite a cook and you're divorced. I hope you took his ass to the mat. Most men don't know how to just let it go. Who cheated? Bet you thought about it."

Morgan blinked her eyes at the barrage of questions. As she started to answer at least one of his questions—yes she could cook—he began to fire off another round.

"You're beautiful, you know that?" he began. "How tall are you? You look kinda short. Do you work out? You've got a nice shape."

She shook her head. Though she wanted to twist her face up into a frown at his answering his own questions, she sat back in her chair and kept her plastered smile.

For almost an hour, Morgan sat and ate in silence as Thomas continued to pepper her with mundane questions, all of which he answered in one breath. She suffered through his endless conversation on what a good catch he was and how no other brother could satisfy a woman quite like he could. All this was coupled with his roving eye—she counted at least three women that he openly flirted with. Morgan was more than ready for their date to end, for she had never met a man quite like Thomas. And she hoped she never would.

Morgan concluded that she did not like Thomas, and knew she wouldn't be caught with him—dead or alive. His brash, up-in-your-face manner and arrogance, coupled with the six gin and tonics he consumed in one hour, danced on her last nerve. The way Morgan saw it, her last nerve was solely reserved for her to tap dance on—her alone.

After calmly enduring another half an hour, Morgan thanked him for the dinner, and then stood to leave. She was stunned when Thomas grabbed her by her left wrist and forcefully pulled her back to her seat.

She slowly picked up the fork, which rested in her plate, and politely stabbed his hand. She hadn't drawn blood, but her action was enough for him to release her wrist.

That's when the night went from bad to worse, bad having left the minute Mr. Thomas "I'm all that" Van Norton had stepped into the restaurant.

When his eyes took on a wild look, Morgan became alarmed and switched modes, calling forth the "street" reserve she readily kept on standby. She stood again, put her hands on her hips, narrowed her eyes and leaned over to whisper in his ear. The verbal tongue lashing she gave Thomas, peppered with a few well placed expletives, worked. Thomas sat back in his chair, gobbled downed his seventh drink, stood quickly, then fell flat.

And that's how she ended blind date number one and found herself rolling along 75th Street, heading to Nick's Sports Bar & Grille.

Morgan smiled as she pulled up in front of the bar. The whole front of the bar had been altered. Gone was the old Pabst Blue Ribbon sign, replaced by a black and white sign with the name of the bar in bold letters. Also, the facing red bricks looked new and the windows were dark, replacing the once clear glass. She nodded her head as a young man, no older than twenty-three, stepped forward and offered to valet her vehicle. Morgan removed her house keys from her ring and handed over her car key. She was impressed when the young man placed his other hand out for her to take and assisted her out of the car. Morgan dug into her purse. The young man put up his hand. "Ma'am, this is complimentary."

She smiled, then nodded her head. "Thank you."

"No, thank you, and please enjoy your evening at Nick's."

She looked up at the beefy bouncer as he held the door for her. "Welcome to Nick's Sports Bar & Grille. I'm Craig. When you are ready to leave, please allow me to escort you outside."

"Thank you, Craig. I'm Morgan. And I will do just that," she replied and batted her eyes as she stepped into the bar and allowed her eyes to adjust to the dimly lit room. She had always liked Nick's, but the renovations had enhanced the establishment, giving it a warm atmosphere, almost comforting, if there was such a thing for a bar that served liquor.

CUPID

Morgan stepped further inside. The old wooden bar had been replaced by a black, marble Formica-topped bar that snaked down the entire length of the room, with bottles of liquor and glasses fastidiously arranged atop several shelves along the back wall. A large mirror stood as the backdrop. Dim lights bounced off the mirror and cast a glowing, almost romantic atmosphere about the establishment. The deep gray walls were painted with various sports figures—the late, great Walter Payton, Julius "Dr. J." Erving, Michael Jordan, and the NHL's first black hockey player, Willie O'Ree, to name a few.

Scented candles dotted atop the deep charcoal colored marble bar with high back, black leather bar stools situated close. Her head bobbed to the old school song, "Love Injection," that blared from the large speakers overhead. Morgan knew the song and thought of the days when she and Yavette club-hopped. She smiled ruefully—that was when she was in her late teens, early twenties. Now thirty-two, she couldn't party like that—dance all night until the sun rose. Morgan walked further into the bar and noticed a larger room to her left. Round tables for four and two, tops marble-like, the color of charcoal grey marble with four matching leather chairs positioned in a semi-circle and facing a large screen television. She closed her eyes briefly and wanted to squeal. Not only was the refurbished Nick's better than before, but she felt she was in pig's heaven—the Bears football game was on. She sat at a table situated in the middle of the room, which afforded her an unobstructed view of the screen, and picked up a menu. Now, only one thing would make her night complete.

Morgan glanced around and was glad to see that Nick's was fairly empty. She guessed that the early hour, coupled with the fact that the bar had just reopened, was the cause for the empty chairs. Yet, after her date with Thomas, she didn't need the often heady conversation she used to engaged in with some of the regulars. On this night, she wanted to see Jarrod, to hear his laughter, to watch his handsome face light up as she told him another one of her dating stories. She had told him of her lack of finding a brother who wanted to settle down, not hit the sack, as so many had assumed. What the few men she had dated after her divorce did not seem to understand was that she was not interested in a one-term night—that she wanted the freedom to change her mind, someone to be with, to possibly go the long haul with. Marriage? She wasn't sure if she wanted to remarry, yet just the same, she wanted to date a brother who wasn't commitment phobic!

She smiled ruefully as she continued to glance around. Jarrod was nowhere in sight, and she began to wonder if he still worked there. He was definitely one of the best reasons she stopped by.

Once she had fantasized about him. In her fantasy, he had come to her and bared his soul, placing his large hands in her small ones. They embraced, and he held her in his arms and whispered words of love and tenderness. She rested her head on his shoulder and felt secure in his touch, his words. And when he brought his lips to rest upon hers, an inferno engulfed her, causing her head to spin deliciously out of control. She could hear herself moan loudly.

But it was just a fantasy, and she had dismissed any thoughts of dating Jarrod. He had never insinuated that there could be any thing more between them than just friends. So, Morgan figured he saw her as just another bar patron—one who couldn't even find a halfway decent date.

"Welcome to the new and improved Nick's. What would you like this evening?" the deep voice asked her, his warm breath close to her neck.

The hairs on Morgan's arms rose, and she could feel the beads of perspiration forming on her brow. She opened her mouth to speak, but quickly shut it as she took in the large form standing over her. His muscular arms strained against the fabric of his black and white striped jersey, which proudly displayed the name of the bar across his wide chest. She smiled brightly as she looked up into Jarrod's light eyes.

"Hey, beautiful." Jarrod smiled as he looked down at Morgan. "I had wondered if you'd heard about the reopening. How've you been?"

Morgan could feel the silly grin on her face as she fought to remain seated, when what she wanted to do was to jump into the arms of this six foot, muscular, 250-pound, chocolate brother whose smile melted her insides and whose intense eyes arrested her good sense. *Now, why couldn't I meet a man like Jarrod?*

Finding her voice, she replied, "I'm great. And the place looks really good, Jarrod. I like the sports arena here. This is really nice."

"Thanks, Morgan. Glad you like it. Can I get you the usual?"

She nodded her head. "You didn't forget." She was sure the beads of perspiration shone on her brow and above her lip like a beacon. Jarrod handed her a napkin. She smiled politely and dabbed at her forehead.

He leaned closer. She could see the depths of his light brown eyes, flecks of gold throughout surrounded by long eyelashes. "How could I forget, Morgan?" He straightened. "I'll be right back. Look over the menu."

Morgan shivered and averted her eyes. The brother was as good going as he was coming. She couldn't resist and turned in her seat. His round head was held high as he walked away, his shoulders as wide as his chest, his derrière solid in a pair of tan khaki's. His physique reminded her of a football player's. Morgan tried to turn back as Jarrod rounded the bar. Too late. He had seen her checking him out. He smiled at her and nodded his head as he retrieved her special glass from the rack from the overhead rack. Embarrassed he had caught her checking him out from behind, she smiled back. As she turned in her seat, her attention was forced onto a blinding, lime green jacket standing in front of her. Her eyes traveled down to matching slacks and shoes.

"Is this seat taken?" Mr. Green Suit inquired. She smirked as the man sat across from her, then stuck his hand out. "Duke. Duke Johnson's the name. And pretty lady, you are?"

Outta here! her mind screamed.

"Morgan."

"Come here often?"

I won't if you are! "I used to. It's my first time back since the renovations."

"Yeah? Well, I use to be a regular back in the day. I heard the family had refurbished, and I wanted to see it for myself. I know the original owner," Mr. Johnson said as he looked around. Morgan thought his brown eyes softened. "Nick Junior really fixed this place up. Looks real nice. Real nice. Don't you think? Oh, here's—"

Mr. Johnson was interrupted when Jarrod appeared and quickly placed the drink in front her, successfully blocking her view of her uninvited tablemate, Duke Johnson. Morgan wanted to laugh.

"Welcome to Nick's. What will you have, sir?" she heard Jarrod ask.

Morgan tried to peer around him. She heard her uninvited tablemate stammer through a drink order. Once Jarrod left, she watched as Mr. Johnson turned around several times, his bushy eyebrows crowded his forehead.

"Strange."

"What?"

"Oh, never mind." Mr. Johnson moved his seat closer to Morgan's. His wide, friendly smile actually warmed her. She smiled back. "So, what's a pretty lady like you doing out alone? Your husband let you out?"

Morgan shook her head and laughed and laughed. She had surmised that her tablemate was at least sixty years old and harmless.

"Mr. Johnson. Sir, I'm not married. I decided to come and see the renovations for myself and was more than happy when I walked inside and saw they had added the sports arenas with the large screens."

"Well, pretty lady…"

"Morgan. Please call me Morgan."

"Morgan it is." He raised his glass. "To the Bears."

Morgan giggled. "To the Bears." They clinked glasses and settled back to watch the game.

Several times, Jarrod returned to her table. Each time Morgan took the opportunity to watch what she had come to term as pure male sensuality. She bet he didn't even know he oozed it. The set of his deep dimples, the pronounced laugh lines around his full lips and the playful glint in his eyes, gave him a blatant, irresistible sexiness. She was slightly disappointed. Before the renovations, she would sit at the bar and talk the night away with Jarrod. She had seen him tonight, but hadn't really spoken to him. Several times, as she listened to Mr. Johnson, she'd glance around and watch him as he mixed drinks. Twice she caught him watching her and nodded his head at her, but he hadn't come over and talked with her like they used to.

At the end of the night, which was closer to 1 A.M., Morgan signaled for the waiter, but was disappointed when a female came to her table. She attempted to pay her bill, but was summarily chided by Mr. Johnson, who pulled several bills from his pocket and paid their bills.

"Thank you. You are too kind."

"No, Miss Morgan. A gentleman never lets a lady pay her own way."

"Again, thank you."

"You have a ride? If not, I'll get Nick to call you a cab."

"Nick?" Morgan stood.

"Yeah, Nick, Jr. He was just here. He's around here somewhere." Mr. Johnson looked around.

Morgan followed his line of vision. She didn't see anyone but the server who had come to collect their tab. She shrugged her shoulders. She wanted to see Jarrod to at least say goodnight. She looked around and didn't see him. She faced Mr. Johnson. "No, sir, that's okay. I drove, but thank you for looking out for me."

"Good. You should come hang out with me on Sundays when the games are on. Or on Thursday night for stepper's night. You can step, can't you?"

Morgan shook her head and laughed. "Aww, Mr. Johnson. I'm from the South Side. We can step."

"Okay, pretty lady. Come step with me Thursday." He took her hand in his and shook it lightly.

Morgan smiled and nodded her head. "I'll think about it, Mr. Johnson. Good night."

"Nite, Miss Morgan."

CHAPTER 2

Jarrod watched as Morgan walked out of the bar, her head held high, her brown twists kissing the nape of her smooth, slender neck. Her stride confident as her generous hips swayed to an orchestrated tune—the beat alone made him want to sway with her. He looked up into her face and smiled when she turned in his direction and waved just before she disappeared from his sight.

He wiped his hands on a cloth, rounded the bar and went over to where she had sat. He hadn't seen her in months, and when she stepped into the bar, he couldn't believe she was there. He had just thought about her and there she stood. He cringed when he thought of the last time he'd seen her. He had finally gotten up enough nerve to ask her out—he had grown tired of listening to her talk about the losers she was dating, when he was who she was looking for. From the first moment she had stepped into the bar nearly a year ago, he had been taken with her. And he used every excuse he could to tend bar every Friday night. He sat across from Mr. Johnson.

"Hey, Mr. Johnson."

"Nicky, mah boy, what was that all about? The winking and stuff?" he asked.

"She doesn't know I own the bar. I didn't want you to give me away. Not yet." He thought about the last woman he'd found attractive who'd sauntered into the bar. She hadn't given him the time of day, even though she had on two wrist watches. Once she found out he was the owner, then she wanted to really get to know him. "I don't really think its important my being the owner. I want her to like me for me."

"But, Nicky, she would not have cared. She seems too down to earth for that type of silliness." Mr. Johnson waved his hand. "Fine. She's going to be my stepping partner."

"I'm telling Mrs. Johnson." Nick laughed. "She's coming back Thursday?"

Mr. Johnson shrugged his shoulders, and then nodded. "Maybe."

Nick turned his head and looked at the space Morgan just vacated. When she first stepped into the bar, he spotted her. He wanted to run right up to her and pull her to him. Instead, he settled for watching her from the one-way mirror, the way her twists hung about her shoulders, the warmth of her smooth cocoa-brown complexion, and the expressive way her dark brown eyes lit up. He had stopped Elena, the server, when she motioned toward Morgan. He kept his eyes on her as he got closer. His head swam when he got a whiff of her perfume—that intoxicating fragrance she always wore that seemed to seep into his pores and held him in a vicious vice-like grip. And when she looked up at him, he noticed she seemed genuinely happy to see him.

He had never been one to fall first—it wasn't in him to do so—but from the first time he saw her, he wanted to talk to her, sit down next to her, stare into her eyes, inhale that heady fragrance. Instead, he settled for serving her drinks and listening to her talk about dating, every once in a while he'd interject, but mostly he just listened to her talk. Hell, he didn't even know what she did for a living or her last name.

"Boy, how's you're dad?" Mr. Johnson interrupted his thoughts.

"Dad's fine. I'm trying to get him to take a vacation. But since mom died, he hasn't wanted to go anywhere." Nick twisted his mouth. The thought of his mother, Lorene, succumbing to Alzheimer's two years ago still hurt his heart.

His mother had been the pillar of the family. When she first began to show the signs of the effects of Alzheimer's, Nick and his two brothers and father had tried to ignore it. After she inadvertently set fire to the house his parents owned since he was born, they could no longer ignore that the Lorene they knew was forever lost to them. His father, Nick Senior, took more time away from the bar to care for Lorene, while Nick and his brothers, Nehemiah and David, pitched in to keep the business running. But unlike his brothers, Nick enjoyed working at the bar. He found the work easy and the people interesting. Everything changed following the death of his mother, and his father no longer seemed interested in the day-to-day operations. Nick decided to quit his job as a financial analyst and took over full time. After a year and much discussion, Nick Jr. bought the bar and decided to renovate.

"Well, give him time. He and Lorene had been together fifty years. Boy, that's longer than most folks can even live nowadays."

"I will. And thanks for coming, Mr. Johnson. Will I see you on Thursday?"

He slapped Nick on his back. "Sure will. And I bet you'll see Miss Morgan, too."

Nick smiled and rose from the seat. "Gotcha, Mr. Johnson. And please do not call me Nick or Nicky in front of her."

Mr. Johnson frowned. "You're making a big mistake. But you young folks think y'all know it all."

"I know, Mr. Johnson. I know. But thanks anyway." Nick patted him on the back. "Hey, you got a ride home?"

"Sure do." Mr. Johnson pointed to his feet and laughed. "But thank you for asking." He rose from his seat, looked up at Nick, and then put his arm around his shoulders. "Your parents did a great job with you and your brothers. Nite, son."

"Nite, Mr. Johnson."

Morgan parked her car in the underground lot, stepped out, then headed to the elevator. She hummed the song she heard as she walked out of Nick's—Jermaine Jackson's "I Know That You Like Me." And as she'd headed toward the exit of the bar, she turned and saw him—Jarrod—smiling at her. She wanted to say something, bye, had a good time, wanna get to know you! Anything, but her feet kept moving her toward the door, and all she did was wave goodbye.

She continued to hum, even sang a few bars off-key as the elevator ascended to the thirty-fifth floor. The soft tone of the floor signal chimed. Morgan stepped off the elevator and headed to her three-bedroom condo. She warmed when she heard the sound of General Patton's persistent mewls, accompanied by the slight whimpers from General Davis.

"I'm here y'all," Morgan whispered as she placed her key in the door. Patton slipped out and rounded her feet as she rubbed her grey body against Morgan's legs. General Davis followed as he placed his small white paws on her legs. Morgan bent over and picked up both pets. She cradled Patton in her left arm and Davis in her right. "Fat cat misses me?" Patton rubbed her face against Morgan's, leaving strands of grey hair on Morgan's cheek. "Thanks. How about you, General Davis?" Morgan scrunched up her face as General Davis gave her a generous licking. "Yuck." She pushed the door closed with her back-side, then placed Patton and General Davis on the parquet floor.

Morgan took off her coat, hung it in the foyer's closet, then slipped off her boots and padded across the hardwood floors to her bedroom. Undressing, she thought of Jarrod. There was something in his eyes, and she hoped she hadn't read anything into his "how could I forget, Morgan," reply. And that body. Surely, he had to know that he was one fine specimen of a man and probably had women lined up all over Chicago trying to get with him. *Naw, I don't need another date*, she told herself, and was instantly reminded that she had two more blind dates to go on, courtesy of the agreement she had made with Yavette, but just the same, if she could get one just like Jarrod it sure would be nice.

Nick rose slowly. His body ached from the week-long activities of getting the bar ready for its grand re-opening. His father had helped, or more like instructed and pointed, as he, Nehemiah and David two brothers, Nehemiah and David, moved tables, carted boxes of beer and liquor, and carried chairs and tables, arranging them according to Nick's request. The work and long hours it took to be ready for the grand re-opening had been grueling, but the end result had been just what Nick had hoped for. Early on the crowd was light, but by night's end, the place was packed. The receipts for the night had totaled nearly fifteen grand.

Nick stretched and swung his long legs over his king-sized bed. He rubbed his head, his close cut hair, and then his eyes. He stretched again and stood. Opening the blinds to let in the late afternoon sun, he glanced around his room. He hadn't cleaned his room, or his house for that matter, in over a month. He turned his nose up as he neared the adjoining bathroom. He had to clean up. Today!

After a shower and a strong cup of coffee, Nick began to clean up his home. He had to admit he was proud of his cleaning abilities. Lorene Chambers had made sure that each of her sons knew how to cook, clean and sew for themselves. She had admonished them on many occasions that a woman who could do those things for them was fine and dandy, but a man who could do for himself showed he had respect for what women had to do to keep home and hearth. As he thought of his mother while he stacked dirty dishes in the dishwasher, Nick smiled sadly. A laugh came to him as he thought of the time he had purchased his mother an automatic dishwasher. She had snorted at the "contraption," insisting that doing the dishes by hand "the old fashioned way" was the best way to get them clean.

Five hours later, Nick had cleaned his entire three-bedroom house, including his smelly bathroom and the basement, which housed his home theatre. He glanced at the clock on the microwave. It was close to seven. He knew Nehemiah would work Nick's tonight, so he didn't need to go to the bar.

Morgan invaded his thoughts. Her warm cocoa skin and deep-set eyes, coupled with that wicked perfume, danced around his senses. He pulled at his goatee and knew that Mr. Johnson was on to something. All the times she had sat at the bar, he knew that she was different. Still, he wanted to make sure that if she liked him, if she'd agree to go out with him, that she was doing so because she wanted to and not because he was the owner. Yet the more he pondered, the more he thought that what he owned shouldn't be important—it was how he treated a person which should be of the utmost importance. And he knew how to treat a woman. He had given Morgan snippets of himself, his wry humor when she failed to see the humor in some of the brothers she had dated, and his sensitivity when he sensed that all she wanted to do was release the steam from some dude playing her like she was silly putty.

Maybe one day soon, he pondered, he'd introduce himself as Nicholas Jarrod Chambers, Junior, the proud owner of Nick's Sports Bar & Grille, instead of Jarrod the waiter-slash-bartender. *But if she likes me, then it won't matter who I am.* Nick paused. *Heck, she may have a boyfriend by now. It has been over six months since I'd last seen her.*

Nick shook loose the thoughts and decided to prepare dinner. He looked into his refrigerator, then smirked as he eyed several bottles of beer, a gallon of water, moldy bread and various other condiments. He hadn't had time to even grocery shop. He shut the refrigerator, then changed into a pair of jeans, a black sweater and his Chamois colored Lugz boots. He grabbed his keys, wallet and cell phone, and then headed out the back door. Once outside, he looked up into the darkening sky. He would have loved to take his motorcycle for a spin, but you can't put grocery bags on a Harley, so he decided to drive his midnight black Mercedes SUV.

Nick's eyes widened as Jermaine Jackson's voice seeped from the car's stereo. It was the same song that played as Morgan walked out of the bar. He shook his head. It was time; he knew it. He just needed to find the right opportunity to tell her how he felt about her. Just like before, she had once again seeped into him and rooted herself. This time, though, he wouldn't make the same mistake twice. When he met and dated Shelia, he had bought her time and affection, and in the end, he felt used and betrayed. But when he met Morgan and they began to talk every Friday night, he found her engaging and genuine and knew she wasn't any thing like his ex. Still, there was one thing he needed to know—and that was her current dating status. Once he knew that, he'd know how to proceed. Until then, he'd settle for what he got—looking at the woman who had gotten under his skin.

Morgan strolled up and down the aisles. She had just finished talking to Yavette, who, though apologetic about Thomas, had unapologetically talked about her next blind date. People in the grocery store had stared at her as she told Yavette about how Thomas ended the date curled up on the steps of the restaurant.

"Wow! I didn't know Thomas was that big of a cad! I'm so sorry," Yavette said. "He definitely misrepresented himself. Talking all that stuff about wanting to settle down and not wanting to play games." Yavette huffed. "Maybe he was nervous. But I've never seen or heard anything out of the ordinary about him. I'm going to definitely speak to him about how he played you; but Morgan, the next one, Tony, should be it. He's really cute and smart."

"Yavette, can't we just skip this one? Don't you agree that Thomas was more than enough?"

"No!" Yavette shrieked into Morgan's ear. Morgan pulled the earpiece from her ear. When she could no longer hear Yavette's voice, she turned the volume down and placed the bud back in her ear. "I'm sorry about Thomas. I swear to you, I didn't know he was like that. But that was just one. You said you'd let me fix you up with three dates. Besides, you gave me your word. And you know…"

"Yes, yes, I know. Word is bond. But Vettie," Morgan used the nickname she had given her first cousin when they were kids, "that's just it. Sometimes for one's own sanity, one's word should be broken."

"Come on, cuz. Just two more dates. Who knows, after you go out with Tony, your dating woes may be over. Heck, you can even disconnect from the Internet."

She thought of the date she had with Laurence next Thursday. She sighed. At least over the phone he seemed to have all his marbles in place. They had been chatting over the Internet for three months before exchanging phone numbers. When Morgan first heard his voice, she struck up an image of a not-too-handsome brother. She and Yavette both had had experiences in their youth where the brother sounded good over the phone, but didn't look as good as he sounded. And though he had sent her a picture of himself, the dark grainy image didn't provide Morgan with a clear picture. But it was his conversation and great sense of humor that eased some of her apprehension, enough to agree to meeting him face to face. That was three weeks ago.

"You still there?" Yavette's voice pulled Morgan out of her temporary reprieve.

"Yeah. Vettie, let me find my own date, will you?"

Yavette sighed. "Come on, Morgan. You haven't had a date in six months. And I think that you and Tony are going to hit it off really well."

"Sure we are." Morgan sighed and rolled her cart down another isle. She looked over her list, then to the items on the shelf. "Yavette, why don't you just give this up? Let me find my own date."

"No, Morgan, no. Give me a chance. I really think this is the one."

"Yavette, you said that about Thomas!" Morgan barked. She laughed when she thought of him lying face down on the restaurant floor. "Besides, I'm not that bad off, so can we skip the next one?"

"Morgan, my favorite cousin."

"I'm the only cousin who's crazy enough to put up with you!"

"No, you're not." Yavette laughed. "But for real. I really think you will like Tony. He's drop dead gorgeous, and he's a manager for one of the city's departments. I met him a couple of months ago when I was working on that trial at the Daley Center. We sat down and talked and there was something about him that was different. He wasn't like most of the brothers out here looking for a quick roll in the hay."

"You thought the same thing about Thomas," Morgan reminded Yavette.

"He misrepresented himself."

Morgan laughed. "That's a nice lawyer term for lied."

"So, okay, shoot me! I struck out with Thomas. But I think you're gonna like Tony."

Morgan listened as Yavette droned on and on about the merits of going out with Tony. Morgan felt Yavette could out-talk anyone and her profession proved it. Yavette was a highly successful trial lawyer. Once, Morgan had gotten the opportunity to see Yavette in action as she defended a client in a wrongful death lawsuit. Morgan had to admit that she was impressed with Yavette's style—slowly moving from one end of the jury box to the other, pausing briefly to look each juror in the eye while she motioned with her hands to emphasize her point. Yeah, that was Yavette's forte. Now if she could just get Yavette out of the matchmaking business.

"So, cousin, what do you say?"

"I say no." Morgan sighed.

"Well, I gave him your number."

"Yavette!"

"I gave him your home office number," Yavette defended. "Aww, come on, Morgan. He's really cute. And a lot of fun. When we went out to lunch the other day, he had me laughing out loud."

"Ooo, I'm telling."

"Oh, Jackson knew all about it. He knows about my trying to find you a date."

Morgan winced. *That's just great. Now Jackson knows, and he's going to think I'm desperate.* "Thanks, Vettie," she replied sarcastically.

"No problem. Anything for you."

Morgan wanted to disconnect the call. Wanted to just plain ol' hang up on her. But she knew Yavette's heart and knew that Yavette felt that she was just being a loving family member and not the pain in the butt she was becoming.

Morgan shook her head as she steered her cart down another aisle. She glanced up, then back to her list, then looked up again. *Unbelievable.* She thought she saw Jarrod stroll past the aisle. Morgan's sneakers made loud squishy noises on the tiled floor as she rushed toward the mouth of the aisle. She turned her head left, then right. He was nowhere in sight. She turned down another aisle. Nothing.

"Did you hear me?" Yavette barked into the phone. "Are you even listening?"

"Umm, ah…"

"Girl, what's the matter?"

Morgan shook her head. Sure, she had thought a lot about Jarrod in the last twenty-four hours. Old feelings had resurfaced upon seeing his warm smile, those show stopping, sexy-as-get-out dimples and that deep, melodic voice that tapped her deep down inside and made her quiver. But she didn't think she had thought that much about him to the point of imagining that she saw him. She shrugged her shoulders. "Nothing. I'm sorry. What were you saying?"

"Well, just in case you don't like Tony, but I think you will, Jackson has a buddy I'd like you to meet."

"Yavette!" Morgan screamed. Several people stole curious glances her way.

"You agreed to three, Morgan. Three. You've only let me fix you up with one. And you know I've been successful at matchmaking. What about Donna and John? And let's not forget about Alicia and Eric. Both are happily married with kids, Morgan. And I think you should give me another opportunity. Thomas defaulted, so technically he shouldn't even count."

"Yavette," Morgan warned. "Two more and that's it!"

Morgan didn't know whether to laugh or cry. But she had to admit that Yavette was quite adept at hooking people up. She had successfully matched their cousin Jason with her friend Donna, and she had matched their other cousin, Alicia with Eric, who was the owner of the apartment building she lived in, but that was over five years ago, but when it came to her she didn't think Yavette knew the right type of man to match her up with.

In the past Morgan had never needed her cousin's matchmaking skills. She was quite successful in finding her own dates, long term ones at that. She and her first boyfriend, Gavin, met during their junior year in high school and dated until one month after they both graduated from college. Following Gavin, Morgan met her ex-husband, Michael, when they both worked for the same advertising agency.

Michael had stepped into the doors of Burrell Communications and had taken the entire place by storm. Quickly rising to Senior Accounts Representative for the entire Midwest region, Michael had stepped to Morgan the first day he walked through the door. And she had been smitten with him, his tall, medium build, café au lait complexion, with a head of wavy curls that lay on his round head. After a year of intense dating, Michael had proposed and Morgan accepted. For five years, Morgan tried to be the kind of wife and woman he wanted, yet it hadn't been enough. When he wanted a showpiece, Morgan had dressed the corporate part. When he wanted a tigress in bed, she had complied, never taking her own passions, her own needs into consideration. The final straw had been when he'd insisted that she quit Burrell to stay home and have children.

And though Morgan had wanted children, she wasn't ready to stay home and birth babies. She had wanted to start her own company, had wanted to explore the world around her—see places outside of Chicago. Michael had never wanted to vacation, always driven to work, always driven by money. Michael had filed for a divorce on their fifth wedding anniversary, citing irreconcilable differences.

Morgan had thought a lot about that fact one night following an intense conversation with Jarrod. He had told her that not all men can be measured with the same measuring stick. As the conversation went on, Jarrod had told her his views on dating, relationships and marriage, which was a plus in Morgan's booking, seeing as how Jarrod was looking to date, wanted a committed relationship and planned to marry. That evening Morgan went home wondering. She had wanted the same things, but as she stood in the isle thinking back on that night so many moons ago, she reminded herself that Michael had said he wanted the same things, too. She knew she couldn't stand another relationship that started out strong, and then fizzled off into nothingness. No, that would just about destroy her, and she didn't want Jarrod to turn out the same way. *Wait, what am I doing? There is no Jarrod and Morgan to worry about.*

"Morgan? Are you paying attention to me?"

"I'm sorry, Vettie, I was taking a trip down memory lane, thinking about Michael."

"Yuck! Why? You've been divorced for four years."

"I know. Just thinking about what type of man I don't want."

"I hear ya, Cuz. Well, I'm thinking of starting my own dating service. If I can hook you up, I know I've got a money maker on my hands."

"What's that supposed to mean?" Morgan whispered into the mike attached to the earpiece.

"Well, you've never really dated. I mean there was Gavin, then Michael. And that's it."

Morgan twisted her face into a scowl. She had always preferred long-term relationships to the maddening dating scene. Yet, since her divorce she'd really struck out in the dating department, shying away from the whole scene based on two dates, of which when she mentioned them to Jarrod, he had cautioned her about her method of measuring. Just to muster up the courage to date took her three years. The only difference now was that Yavette was matching making.

When Morgan thought about it, she really had little to no experience with the opposite sex. She was no virgin, but she also didn't know passion, hadn't had her toes curled. According to their cousin Alicia, it wasn't passion if your toes didn't curl and she claimed her husband curled her toes on a regular basis. Morgan felt dumb. She didn't even know what it meant to have her toes curled, much less any of the other things Alicia had talked about the last time she had spent the day with Morgan and Yavette. Yavette laughed and Morgan snickered like a schoolgirl, yet she hadn't experienced any of the things Alicia and Yavette were talking about. Outside of a steamy romance novel or two, things like that never happened to Morgan. Morgan had been a two-man woman; one she dated in college, the other, she married. That was the extent of her experience and neither had "curled her toes." But

Yavette always had plenty of boyfriends, not saying she slept with any of them, but there was always a person lingering around, yet Yavette and a date never lasted more than three months. But Jackson, her latest beau, had outlasted them all. Morgan tilted her head to the side. Yavette had always dismissed her beaus for one reason or another, but Jackson seemed to have staying power. They had been dating for a year.

"Hey, what's up with Jackson?"

"Oh, his friend is a dream and is fine! Built like the Rock. I've met him. His name is—"

"No," Morgan interrupted. "I don't mean the friend. I'm talking about Jackson? How's he doing?"

"Oh, Morgan." She heard Yavette sigh dreamily. "We've got to sit down and talk. And I don't think I want to wait until tomorrow. How about tonight?"

Morgan raised her right eyebrow. The last time Yavette needed an "emergency" sit down was years ago when she wanted Morgan's advice on a job offer that would require she move to Los Angeles. After much discussion, Yavette decided to stay in Chicago. Outside of that, they always got together early Sunday morning for some Pilates, followed by a light lunch and a trip to their hair stylist. Most Saturdays, like this one, Morgan spent a few hours in the office, then headed home for a date with a box of Chicken Chow Mien, Showtime and her dog and cat, the Generals Davis and Patton, respectively.

"Sure, Vettie. I've got to make two more stops. I should be home in a few hours. If I'm not there when you arrive, use your key."

"Okay. I'll see you later."

"See ya. I love ya."

"Love you, too."

CHAPTER 3

Nick made quick work of grocery shopping. His large feet strolled quickly down each aisle as he tossed items from his list into the shopping cart. He started to roll the cart past one aisle when out of the corner of his eye he thought he spied Morgan. He stopped, backed up, and peered down the aisle. He rolled back to the aisle to his left. No sign of her. He rolled the cart forward. Still no sign.

"Boy, you're tripping," Nick whispered as he returned to his shopping, wondering what in the world had gotten into him to make him hallucinate an image of Morgan. True, he had thought about her on and off throughout the day. It was great seeing her again, but to conjure up images was absurd.

At the checkout counter, he smiled pleasantly at the cashier who made it quite clear with her eyes, which openly stared at him as he waited behind a customer, that she was interested. Once it was his turn, the cashier engaged him in small talk. He glanced at her nails, which were, in his opinion, a bit too long, a bit too overly painted, with tri-colors and sparkles on each talon. He looked up her arm full of gold bracelets, past her tight, red smock to her hair, which was at least six inches tall and pasted a tad bit too close to her head. He looked at her face. A sweet face, he guessed her to be no more than twenty-one, but she had on too much makeup, mascara clumped on her long lashes. Besides, she was much too young for his taste.

"Thank you for shopping at Save More. Please come again." The cashier smiled as she looked at Nick's receipt. She batted her eyes as she looked up into his. "Mr. Chambers."

"Thank you." Nick looked at the cashier's name tag. "Tanzaneeka. I will."

"And when you do, by all means, allow me to assist you." She batted her eyes and smiled broadly. As Nick began to leave, he felt a hand on his arm.

"But if you would like to take me out," Tanzaneeka placed a folded piece of paper in his hand, "just ring me." He smiled politely as he watched her walk back to her register. Her more than ample hips swung viciously from east to west. Nick didn't want to be rude, but she had just too much rump to bump. He just nodded his head and left the store.

Nick piled the plastic bags holding his groceries into the rear cab of the SUV. He remembered what sack the bagger placed his Oreo cookies in, fished out the blue and white package and tossed the cookies to the front seat. As he returned the cart, his cell phone rang. He looked at the caller ID.

"What's up, Jackson?"

"You, man. Sorry I had to miss the grand re-opening last night. How'd it go?"

"Man, it was great. We had a really good crowd. Between the regulars and the new folks just wanting to check out the place, we made a killing."

"Glad to hear it. Hey, where you at?"

"I had to pick up some stuff at the grocery store. Felt like practicing my culinary skills and didn't have a damn thing to practice with."

"Oh, my brother. What cha cookin'?"

Nick laughed. "Naw, Jack. You need to go on over to your girl's." Nick heard Jackson laugh.

"Awright, be like that. Hey, what cha doing tomorrow? Feel like a little ass kicking on a court?"

"Ahh, I see brother got jokes. How large of a can?"

"Can?"

"Yeah, can," Nick responded. "How large of a can of kick ass shall I bring with me."

The pair broke out into raucous laughter. It had been several weeks since the two had played basketball. Between Nick preparing for the reopening of the bar and Jackson with his girl, Yavette, neither had made time to get together for their Sunday basketball ritual.

"Aww, man you wrong for that." Jackson chuckled. "How about 8:30?"

"Sounds good to me. If the weather is crappy, we'll do Apollo Park. If not, we'll meet up at 31st Street. Cool?"

"Alright, old man. Just don't forget your pillow."

Nick laughed. "Sure. But for real, how you been?"

"Good. And I know I've been a little MIA lately. But, man, when a brother's got a good woman, what can I say?"

"I hear ya, man. No trip on my part. So how is the lovely Miss Yavette?"

Nick climbed into his SUV and started it up. He began to back out.

"Doing well. How's Tanya?"

Nick heard Jackson chuckle, but he wasn't amused. He thought about Tanya, his last date and Jackson's co-worker at the Department of Child Services. Jackson had told him that she was cute, sweet natured, had a body to kill for and had arranged for them to meet. Well, she was cute and she had a show-stopping body, but to hell if she was sweet. After two dates, Tanya had started talking about children and marriage, and they hadn't even slept together. Sure, he wanted to get married, even wanted to father a few children, if he was so blessed to do so, but he did not see Tanya as the one. So when he begged off seeing her again, the woman went ballistic and started following him and calling him on every electronic device he had day and night. One night he had to call the cops after a brick incident—big brick, wrong window. She broke the neighbor's window instead of his. In the end, Nick wanted to strangle Jackson instead of Tanya.

Umm, naw, he thought, *absolutely no more blind dates.* Besides, Jackson couldn't pick women for him. Jackson was the one who was lucky in love; Jarrod was not.

"Jackson, my brother I gotta jet. I'll call you in the morning."

"Wait. I need to tell…"

"Naw, gotta go. Bye," Nick interrupted, then disconnected the call. He had an odd feeling that Jackson had more to say on the subject of dating, but he wasn't interested in hearing a damn thing he had to say. Besides, Nick had other things on his mind: namely Morgan. During the months of renovations, he'd wondered about her. The day of the re-opening, he'd hoped that she would show. And when she sauntered through the door, he knew his prayers had been answered.

Nick looked at his watch. It was half past eight in the evening. He pulled into his driveway and smiled when he spotted his younger brother, David, sitting on the steps of his porch.

They clasped hands and embraced once Nick stepped out of the car. Even though David was two years younger, Nick often found himself seeking his advice. Besides, out of the three of them, David was the most level headed. Always seeing things clearly. And as kids, they were inseparable.

Nick looked at David. He looked the most like their mother. "What's up, baby boy?"

"Not a whole lot. What's up with you?"

Nick rounded the vehicle and opened the hatch. "Just got back from the store."

"You cooking tonight?" David grinned.

"What's up with you and Jackson? He just called me asking about food. Don't y'all's women cook?"

"Mine's all good. But she went out with her girlfriends tonight." David smiled. "Now, she wanted to cook me something, but I refused, gave her some money and told her to have a nice time—that I was coming over here to bug the hell out of you."

Nick chuckled. "Well, that's awfully black of you, my brother."

"That's how you keep a woman happy. Spoil her rotten. You should try it sometime. Find you a good woman."

"Yeah, right," Nick said as he rolled his eyes and thought how easy it was for him to say. His jaw became taunt as he thought of Sheila and how he *had* spoiled her. She just didn't appreciate it.

Admittedly, his instincts had told him that they weren't meant to be. She didn't like the time and energy he put into the business, and he didn't like the way she openly flirted with other men when they were together. Model beautiful, Sheila thought that Nick needed to become a suit and tie brother, putting his MBA to corporate use, not "some bar keeper in a watering hole." Never mind that Nick also owned a healthy investment portfolio of real estate and was a silent partner of a popular spa resort named Serenity.

Jackson and David had both tried to give him gentle hints that Sheila was out for herself. And a part of him knew that she hadn't loved him outside of the last gift he gave her. Yet, for some inexplicable reason back then, Nick couldn't seem to let her go. He crazily thought that maybe if he gave her everything she wanted,, tended to her every financial whim, that she would love him without pause. Love him unconditionally. Still, the more he did for Sheila, the more she wanted and seemed never satisfied. He knew he was being a chucklehead, what his oldest brother, Nehemiah, termed as the equivalent of a female chicken head, but Nick couldn't help it. He had loved the way her dark eyes lit up when he presented her with yet another present. The way she would lay her supple body on his. But the final straw for Nick was when she asked him to sell the bar and invest the proceeds in a business idea of hers.

The bar had been a part of him—his life. There would be no way he'd sell Nick's, his father's legacy. In the end, Sheila had given him an ultimatum—sell the bar or they were finished.

For months afterwards, Nick wanted nothing to do with women— oh, he loved women, loved the intricate and beautiful hues his black sisters came in, but he just couldn't get with the games—the emotional roller coasters some women could put you on and try like hell never to let you off. And Sheila was one hell of a ride. Still, he foolishly thought he had loved her thoroughly and completely. Eventually, he came to understand that ego was a motha', and he had let his lead and rule his common sense. That was three years ago.

"Man, I said spoil, not buy. Anyway, that's old news. Any new sistahs on the horizon?"

Nick thought of Morgan. Her warm brown eyes and that wicked perfume. In spite of himself, he smiled.

"Aww, big brother. What's her name?"

Before he could stop himself, he called out her name. "Morgan."

"Where'd you meet her? What's she like? Give up the goods."

Nick suddenly felt foolish. At thirty-nine, he felt he had outgrown crushes and love at first sight. Yet how could he explain the emotions he felt for Morgan? The first time she stepped into Nick's he'd been taken with her, but he hadn't had the nerve to ask her out. Now she was back.

"Not a whole lot to tell. She came into the bar last night and sat with old man Johnson."

"Aww naw, not the one and only Duke Johnson—the ol' school pimp? Brother, was he mackin'?" David laughed.

"Hard." Nick laughed. He thought about what Mr. Johnson had said. He didn't think she'd be interested in him, a bartender.

"When are you and Miss Morgan going out?"

Nick avoided his brother's steady gaze. There was no way he was going to admit that he'd known her for some time, but hadn't had the nerve to asked for her number, much less for a date. If his brothers knew, they'd disown him, for the Chambers men always went after what they wanted. He grabbed a grocery bag.

David cocked his head to the right and squinted his eyes. "Well?" He reached into the rear hatch and pulled out several grocery bags, leaving Nick with two bags and his open package of Oreo cookies.

"Well, what?"

David stood in front of Nick. "You didn't get her number?" Nick could see the frown on David's face as he shook his head no. He watched as David turned and walked up the porch steps. Nick followed, then stepped around him and unlocked the door. Once inside, David headed straight for the kitchen while Nick disarmed his home security system.

Nick came up behind his brother and watched as he poked his head in the refrigerator. He was relieved that his brother had dropped the subject. But he also knew better. David was just giving him time to absorb the absurdity of it all.

"Yeah, boy, this joke is empty! I can hear crickets." David laughed at his own joke as Nick began to put away his groceries. "I thought mom taught you better." David retrieved a beer from the refrigerator. "What's on the menu tonight?"

"You'll see. By the way, have you talked to Nehemiah today?"

"No, you?" David took a sip of his beer.

"No, but I think he and Cara are on the outs again."

"Jesus, what gives with those two? They forever mad at each other. I don't know why he married her in the first place." David hadn't liked Cara from the moment he met her. He had told Nick that the woman came on to him, and when he tried to tell Nehemiah, he had waved him away and said that Cara was just overly flirtatious. David hadn't said another word, and neither had Nick when he spotted her on the arm of a brother—not his brother.

"I hear ya. Dad said he spent the last couple of nights with him. And he was a little too anxious to tend bar tonight."

David shook his head. "When's he going to see that she just ain't for him? She's never home. And have you been to their apartment lately? It looks like a hurricane blew through there. Nehemiah used to clean up, but even he's adopted the slovenly look."

Nick nodded his head and though about their older brother. Forty years old, Nehemiah had been a serious playboy up until he met Cara. David nor Nick had cared for the numerous games Nehemiah liked to play with women. And when they'd mention it to him, Nehemiah would question their sanity and implored them to, "Try it—y'all might like it."

Neither took their older brother up on his offer. David was in love with his high-school sweetheart, Alexis, whom he married right after high school and had been with ever since. As for Nick, he had never been interested in gratuitous sex. Wasn't his bag. Besides, his mother had always told all of them to never lay with a woman you wouldn't mind spending the rest of your life with—tomorrow comes. Now he was far from a virgin, had had his share of women, just not as many as his brother Nehemiah claimed to have had.

Nick sighed heavily and thought of Nehemiah's wife. The sister had a bodacious body—one that men dreamed of, and had a pretty, peach shaped face the color of rich mocha. Nehemiah and Cara had met at a bar, slept together that night and had been an item ever since. Cara was what brothers called "easy," and Nick couldn't understand why Nehemiah chosen to put up with her less than scrupulous ways.

Maybe the family joke about Nehemiah was true: they had found him on the door step. He faced David. "Do me a favor? Go out to the yard and start up the grill." Nick grabbed a set a keys from a kitchen drawer and tossed them to David. "The grill and charcoal are in the garage."

Nick finished putting away his groceries, then removed pots and pans to begin his dinner. He picked up the phone and dialed the bar.

"Nick's Sports Bar and Grill. Nehemiah speaking."

"What's up? How are things?" Nick asked over the background noise of voices and music.

"Can barely hear you. Let me change phones. Hold on." Several moments later, the extension was picked up. "That's better. All's good. We've got a heck of a crowd tonight. I think you're gonna top out again, my brother."

"Sounds good. Need me to come in?"

"Naw, I can handle this. I need the distraction."

Nick shook his head. "You okay?"

"Nope. But I don't wanna talk about it right now. Look, I've got your business to run. I gotta jet. I'll come by in the morning with your receipts."

"Got ya. Don't come without the green." Nick heard Nehemiah laugh just before he hung up on him.

Nick depressed the button again and called his father. He listened to the message. As always, he grew solemn when the outgoing message played—it was his mother's voice. At the sound of the beep, he swallowed hard before he spoke. "Dad, it's Nick. I'm grilling and David is here. Come on by if you get this message." Nick placed the cordless receiver on its base. He had talked to his father about replacing the outgoing message. His response had been the same for each of them. "Mind your own damn business." And that's just what they each did. Still, it was odd to hear his mother's light and cheery voice and not be affected by it.

He shook loose the emotions and returned to preparing tonight's meal: grilled T-bone steaks, baked beans, twice-baked garlic potatoes and vegetable kebabs, marinated in a sweet and spicy peanut sauce.

After an hour, just as Nick and David sat on the back deck to eat, their father appeared with a case of beer in one hand and a cake in the other.

"Do I have great timing, or what?" Nick Senior stepped up on the deck. Nick and David both stood and each embraced their father.

"Let me put the beer in the fridge and grab me a plate. Don't start without me."

"I'm starvin' like Marvin," David began. "I don't wanna wait."

Nick laughed and thought how much he sounded like he did when they were kids. Their mother always insisted that they wait for their father to have dinner, and no one could eat a morsel unless their father was present at the head of the table.

Nick watched in rapt amazement as David picked up his steak knife and began slicing through the tender meat. As he went to place a morsel in his mouth, he looked up with a stunned expression plastered on his face as the fork he had been holding was slapped from his hand. "What the..."

"Boy, didn't I tell you to wait for me? Greedy child." Nick Sr. sat between them. "And I bet you heathens haven't even blessed your food. Bow your heads."

They complied. At the sound of "Amen" David looked at Nick and smirked. "Can I eat now, Reverend Ike?"

Nick laughed and began eating. The cordless phone next to him rang.

"Hello," Nick spoke into the handset. He nodded his head. "Okay, call Mr. Johnson. His number is on my desk in the Rolodex. Have him fix the leak and pay him in cash." Nick shut off the phone.

"Is there anything wrong?" Nick, Sr. asked.

"Nothing that Mr. Johnson can't fix. There's a leak in the second sink in the kitchen."

Nick looked at the man he was named after. They shared many of the same features, the smooth deep, chocolate complexion, the broad nose, and deep set dimples. They were even built alike.

"Smart choice. Duke's good. Did I ever tell y'all the story of the case of liquor?"

Nick and David laughed and listened as their father went on to tell the infamous story of the two of them running down a Northside alley with two crates of liquor each and undercover Drug and Alcohol agents chasing them, but not able to catch them. It was one of their father's favorite stories. And though they had heard this one a thousand times over, they let their father tell it anyway, never interrupting him when parts of the story changed to suit the mood. Besides, Mr. Duke Johnson had been a part of their family for as long as Nick could remember. He couldn't recall ever a time when there wasn't a Mr. Johnson.

"Boy, that sure was some meal." Nick, Sr. leaned back and patted his stomach. "You haven't cooked in a month of Sundays."

"I know. Been too busy."

"David, go get me a beer."

David disappeared into the house. Nick watched his father. The pensive look on his face told him that he had something important to say. "Have you talked to Nehemiah?"

"Yeah, that was him on the phone. And I talked to him earlier when I called to check on the bar."

"Then y'all haven't had a chance to really talk."

Nick stood and gathered the paper plates and cups. He tossed them into the large rubber garbage receptacle on the porch, then came back and sat across from his father. "No. What's wrong this time?"

"That boy, I swear we found him on the front porch." Nick Senior chuckled, but stopped short when he saw the troubled expression on his son's face. "Cara's pregnant."

"Hey, isn't that great news? I've always wanted to be an uncle."

"I ain't the grandpa. And you and David aren't gonna be uncles."

Nick tilted his head to the side and narrowed his eyes. He didn't want to register the words his father had just spoke, for if he did, then it would mean that Nehemiah's wife had committed the ultimate crime–slept with another man. And to add to it, she was pregnant. *Dang!* Nick shook his head and thought of his brother. "That's deep. What is wrong with her?"

His father shrugged his shoulders. "No, the real question is: what is wrong with the both of them? He said he's filing for divorce."

Divorce. That was a foreign word in the Chambers household. Their parents had married at twenty-one and stayed together until his mother died. Nick knew that once he married, he would remain so until he breathed his last breath.

"Who's filing for a divorce?" David asked as he returned to the deck.

"Nehemiah. Seems as if his wife's ways have finally dawned on him. She's pregnant, and he isn't the father."

"What the …?" David began as he sat down heavily in the chair. He handed Nick and their father a beer. "How does he know?"

"He said they haven't had relations in over six months, and he noticed she was getting a little thick around the waist. When he questioned her about it, she told him it was the rich foods they had been eating at various restaurants. Neither of them can cook worth a damn. But when he caught her throwing up one morning, he said he knew." He took a hefty sip from his bottle of beer, then sat the bottle down. "Let me tell you both something. Marriage is a serious thing. Your mother and I didn't raise y'all to act like whores, passing your penis around like it's a lifeline. And we most certainly didn't give y'all the last name of mat—and neither of y'all's first name is 'door.'"

In spite of the seriousness of their conversation, David and Nick couldn't help but chuckle. Their father had always preached this sermon to them for as long as they could remember.

"Dad, you don't have to worry about me," David said. "Alexis is straight."

"I know that. Knew it when you brought her by." He looked at his namesake. "What about you?"

"What about me? I'm not married."

"So? Just because you're not married doesn't give you license to go out here and chase every skirt that passes you by. Not all skirts are meant to be lifted. As men, we have to respect our women. Be discriminate and not mess with their heads and hearts. We have to uphold our women and not degrade them by treating them like objects." He paused and looked at his sons. "'Cause if you do, they'll certainly show you a thing or two. Just like Cara. Some man done treated that woman wrong, and she's out to make some sort of statement."

"Dad, there's no one serious," Nick replied.

"Well, what happed to that brick thrower?"

The three of them looked at each other, then broke into a raucous laugh. "Truly, you didn't want Tanya as a daughter-in-law?" Nick said.

"Naw, but we could have signed her up with the Green Bay Packers. She had quite an arm." Nick Senior chuckled.

As their laughter quieted, Nick watched as his father turned serious once again. "And we don't even need to talk about Sheila. I know she wasn't the woman for you, son. But when you find that right woman, you'll know it. You won't be able to get her out of your senses—out of your head. When that happens, like it did for me with your mother, you'll know. And you will move heaven and hell to keep her."

Nick simply nodded.

For the rest of the evening, Nick sat with his father and brother and discussed life, love and living to the fullest. He enjoyed the closeness he shared with them, and wished Nehemiah was here.

CUPID

He thought of Morgan. She was in his senses, her perfume stamped into his memory, her face plastered into his mind. He wondered if this was what his father meant, and was he ready to move heaven and hell to get her.

CHAPTER 4

Morgan lightly smoothed her hand across the champagne gold Formica top of the center island, then allowed her eyes to take in the look of the expansive kitchen, painted antique white. It was one of the major selling points for her. When she had first entered the upper story condo, she wasn't too sure about purchasing a condo in the heart of the downtown Chicago, yet when she stepped inside and witnessed the spacious layout of the living room, with its magnificent fireplace and the unobstructed eastern view of Lake Michigan, she was sold. She placed a bid on the unit right then, and there.

After she bought the three-bedroom Condo, Morgan took six months to decorate her new home to fit her personality. She had each room re-painted. Antique white for her kitchen; a wicked burnt orange for her sitting room, which doubled as her home office; taupe for the guest room; and a deep red on one wall, cream on the remaining ones, for her bedroom, which held a large, wrought-iron canopy bed with long sheer scarves draped over each end.

Morgan put away her groceries, then leaned against the kitchen island. She wasn't sure if she wanted to cook or order her favorite Chinese take out. She thought of the can of Sockeye Salmon, removed the can from an overhead cabinet and placed it on the island. She then opened a narrow door situated on the side of the island. When Morgan had first spotted the narrow cabinet, she wasn't sure what to do with it. But following a happily expensive trip to the Container Store, she had found two sliding drawers, which she installed herself. The drawers now held some of her favorite CDs. She selected a CD, placed it into the under-the-cabinet CD/radio player, then selected the song she wanted to hear. She closed her eyes and nodded her head as the sounds of a soothing flute introduced Yanni's "Love Is All," from his Tribute CD.

She opened the can and smiled as Patton, followed by General Davis, came rushing out of nowhere. Davis, her finicky snoozer, didn't like fish, but Patton, true to her feline nature, loved it and could smell fish a block away.

"Okay, here." Morgan placed a few flakes in Patton's bowl. She looked at General Davis. "You don't like fish," she spoke to the dog as she rummaged through another cabinet and retrieved a package of doggie treats. "Here. I know you hate being left out."

She emptied the can's contents into a bowl, adding bread crumbs, cracker crumbs, a little Worcestershire sauce, an egg, and onions and green peppers that had been sautéed in butter.

After nearly an hour, Morgan had completed her meal of croquettes with a hollandaise sauce, white rice and asparagus, flavored with lemon pepper. She looked at the clock and knew that Yavette should have arrived by now.

She thought about Nick's Sports Bar and Grille and Jarrod: his wicked smile, beautiful, intense eyes, deep dimples and well-fitting khakis.

The ringing sound of her telephone broke Morgan from her temporary reverie. She grabbed the phone, heard Yavette's voice, and then hit several buttons that would allow her cousin to enter the building.

As she waited for Yavette's knock on the door, it suddenly hit her— the reason why Yavette was so hell bent on finding her a date. Yavette wanted her to be as happy as she was. Yavette, who wasn't one for bars, had met her current beau, Jackson, at a black-tie fundraiser given to support women who've suffered from domestic violence. Morgan had attended the same fundraiser, but hadn't noticed Jackson until he approached Yavette. She thought him handsome, with his clean-shaven head, his full lips and his cinnamon complexion—just Yavette's type of man.

That was over a year ago, and the fire between them still raged strong. Morgan sighed. Yes, she wanted that type of passion, but she didn't want it from a brother who would fake it just to get her into bed. No, she wanted a real love—one that would creep into your senses, make you say crazy things and howl at the moon.

Again, she thought about Jarrod and wondered if he knew passion, both personally and professionally. If he had, maybe he wouldn't be tending bar. Then again, he may be doing it as a side job. His real job was somewhere in corporate America. Yeah, right. A brother working in corporate America wasn't hardly going to tend bar, no matter how nice the establishment. Maybe he owned the place. But would that really matter? All that mattered to her was how he treated her, not how he made his living. *Then again, Dad would have a fit.* She thought about her father, who, as a minister, condemned all drinking and saw dating as a precursor to marriage. He'd have a stroke if he knew that she was going out on Internet dates, commit her if he knew she had allowed Yavette to fix her up on blind dates and kill her for dating a man who sold the "devil's brew."

Reverend Ishmael Paige knew his daughter had to entertain clients, which called for her to go to restaurants that served liquor, but he hadn't a clue that for every Friday for several months she sat on a bar stool in then Nick's Sports Bar and Grille and sipped a beverage with alcohol in it. Morgan sighed heavily at that thought. And though she and her father were close, she'd chosen not to tell him.

The sound of knocking on her door pulled her from her thoughts. She walked from the kitchen and peered through the peephole, but could see nothing.

"Girl, take your finger away from the peep hole," Morgan said as she opened the door. She smiled as Yavette strolled into the foyer, holding a brown bag and her overnight case.

"Here," Yavette handed her a bag. "Brought us some sparkling cider."

"Too bad it's not Boone's Farm."

They laughed. Yavette wiped the tears from her eyes as she stepped into the foyer. "Girl, don't ever mention that again! I thought Uncle Ishmael was going to kill me."

Morgan nodded as she recalled the one and only time she had ever been drunk.

At fifteen, she and Yavette had paid some stranger two dollars to buy them a bottle of wine. They took their wine and went to the neighborhood park and sat on a bench and drank the wine from a brown paper bag. After consuming the entire bottle, the pair stumbled and stammered to Morgan's house. Though it had been Morgan's idea, Yavette got the blame for getting them both drunk off of Boone's Farm. Morgan had never been sicker, but she also had never seen her father angrier.

The pair embraced. Upon releasing Yavette, Morgan rolled her overnight case into the guest room. "Guess you're spending the night," she said as she returned to the living room and walked over to Yavette, who was standing at the large window. She looped her arm through Yavette's and led her to the formal dining room. "Food's ready."

Morgan had set the table with her best china. She'd read an article reportedly from Erma Bombeck shortly before the witty columnist died from complications for a kidney ailment which extolled living life to the fullest. Ever since, Morgan had insisted on using the best and tried to see richness and humor in everything—including her cousin and her crazed idea of hooking her up on blind dates.

She placed food on Yavette's plate before serving herself, then sat across from her. They bowed their heads just before they dug into the delectable food.

"Girl, this will make you slap your momma," Yavette moaned as she chewed a morsel of the croquette.

"Yeah, but your momma will slap you back."

Yavette's mother and Morgan's father were siblings in a throng of eight—five boys and three girls—highly religious and fiercely protective of their clan.

"Okay, maybe not slap Etta, but certainly make me want to smart off just before I run."

The pair laughed and fell into an easy conversation. Morgan was enjoying her cousin's banter, and she listened intently as she talked about work and Jackson. Her face twisted into a scowl when Yavette asked her if she was ready for her next blind date.

"Of course I'm not!"

"Come on. I've already told him that you're going to go out with him."

Morgan stood quickly. "You've what?" She quickly cleared the dishes from the table and headed into the kitchen. She heard Yavette's footsteps behind her.

"I called him after I talked to you," Yavette said. "Look, you promised me three dates. And like I told you, Tony's really cute. I don't think there'll be another blind date. He's really interested in you."

"In me or Paige Incorporated?"

"Of course I told him what you do. That's standard fare."

"Yavette." Morgan sighed as she faced her cousin. "I really need to break my word on this. Thomas was more than enough."

"No." Yavette took Morgan's hand in hers. "Like I said, he misrepresented himself. He had me believing that he was looking for a serious relationship. On Monday morning, I'm going to have to talk with Mr. Van Norton. But let me tell you about Tony…"

Morgan became silent as Yavette went on to describe Tony Martin, her next blind date. From Yavette's description, Morgan was only vaguely interested and hadn't cared in the least that he was a manager in one of the City of Chicago's countless departments. He could be the mayor for all she cared. Her thoughts raced to Jarrod. She shook her head, trying to release the images of him standing in front of her with his sexy smile and twinkling eyes.

"So, Morgan, how about it?" Yavette interrupted Morgan's daydream.

"Umm? What did you say?"

"You're not listening to me, are you?"

"Yes I am. When's the date?"

"You know me well." Yavette laughed. "Whenever you two decide. Here's his phone number. He's looking forward to meeting you."

"I just bet he is."

Morgan shook her head as they settled in for the evening. The pair walked into the den and turned on the television. Yavette smiled as General Davis strolled into the room and jumped up into her lap. After stretching wildly, General Davis aptly rested himself squarely on her lap. Yavette began to scratch behind the dogs ears. They both laughed as the dog's small tail thumped wildly on Yavette's thigh.

Patton preferred the back of the couch.

"Jackson asked me to marry him last night."

Morgan paused. Yavette, never married, had always been there for her. She had been there when she married Michael and had helped her pick up the pieces when she and Michael divorced. Morgan looked at Yavette and felt a twinge of jealousy. And though Morgan couldn't recall a time when Yavette had ever been dateless, she also couldn't recall a time when Yavette hadn't dismissed one of her dates; whereas, Morgan liked commitment and wasn't a fan of the dating scene. She'd had two boyfriends, one of whom she married. She thought about that. Maybe if she had dated more, like Yavette, had gone out with a variety of brothers, then maybe she wouldn't be so at wits' end about this whole blind date/dating thing.

She focused her attention on the concern stretched across Yavette's face. She took her hand in hers. "You should be ecstatic. What's the matter, Vettie?" Morgan's eyes widened as she watched her cousins warm brown eyes well up with tears. "Oh, girl," Morgan crooned as she snatched several tissues from a nearby dispenser, handed them to Yavette, then pulled her into her arms. "Tell me what's wrong."

Yavette sniffed loudly before she blew her nose into the tissues. She shifted from Morgan's embrace and looked her cousin in the eye. "I'm afraid, Morgan."

Morgan smiled and nodded. She understood the fear—had tried to keep it at bay several times, to no avail. "Why are you afraid?"

"I've never loved anyone like I love Jackson. And we haven't ..." she stopped.

"Haven't what?"

Morgan studied Yavette. She could see there was something she wanted to say, but the words never came forth as the tears rolled down her cheeks.

Morgan took her hands. "There's nothing to be afraid of. I know you love Jackson. I can tell by the way you two look at each other, the uncanny way the two of you finishes the other's thoughts and the way your eyes sparkle when you mention his name."

"You see all that?"

"Yes," Morgan said as she nodded her head. "You're going to be a great couple, and you are going to be a wonderful wife to him."

Yavette wiped a lone tear and smiled. "You think so?"

"I know so, sweetie. Don't worry."

"Will you be my maid of honor?" She sniffed.

Morgan smiled. "Who else will put up with you?" She embraced her cousin again.

"And will you go out with Jackson's best friend?" Yavette looked up.

"You're asking too much," Morgan sneered. "No," she replied, and then gave Yavette a terse look. She watched as the resignation crossed over her cousin's eyes, but she also knew that this wasn't the end of their conversation, not by a long shot.

The alarm clock blared as Nick swung his muscular legs over the side of the bed. He hit the clock with such force that it tumbled from the nightstand to rest atop the heap of his clothes strewn carelessly beside the bed. He rubbed his eyes, stretched wildly, then stood. *That Morgan!* He sighed. After David and his dad left, he had thought about her for the rest of the night. The warmth in her deep voice, the animation in her eyes as she talked.

When he first saw her, he thought of Jermaine Jackson's song, "I Know That You Like Me." He didn't understand at first, but when he listened to the song, memorized the lyrics, he knew why. The sultry tune asks does she like him, too. Pure and simple.

He knew that Morgan was searching, searching for someone to take her seriously, be by her side—to love her. Nick guessed that she was tired of the dating scene, and he couldn't much blame her. He was tired too. Tired of the baggage that women unfortunately brought with them from previous relationships. He was sick of what he considered the Chicken Head Review, and the women who subscribed always expected him to play along without protest.

At thirty-nine, the last thing Nick wanted was another game playin' sister. He had met one too many and decided instead to give the bar his full attention.

Sure, he'd had a couple of dates over the past several months, which included Tanya, the one whom Jackson had fixed him up with. But each date left him wondering about one woman: Morgan Paige. He remembered how she had waltzed her beautiful self into the bar, sat down, sipped her drink and talked to him like a long time buddy, telling him all about her dates. And when she had, he had taken her hands in his, the softness of them, and the pained uncertainty in her eyes, struck him deep. Yet, she had tried to mask the pain with her rich laughter and witty verbiage. The touch, to him, was his way of trying to comfort her, but it also left him empty and wanting. And he knew then that he didn't want to hear about any other man taking her out! He didn't want to be her damn buddy, either! He wanted to be her man.

Why sweat it? She thinks I'm just another bartender anyway. Besides, a woman like Morgan wouldn't want to date a bartender. She had not one clue as to who he really was—the owner of Nick's Sports Bar & Grille. *No,* his thoughts tumbled. *She has to want me for me, not the owner of Nick's.*

Named after his father, Nick had started working in the bar after his mother's diagnosis. After she died, he took a leave of absence from his job to run the bar full time. A year later, he purchased the bar and then refurbished it six months later. He wanted to make the bar the kind of establishment that older black professionals could frequent without having to deal with the nuisance of a younger crowd. He decided not to rename the bar—especially since it stood as a testament to the man whose name he shared: Nicholas Jarrod Chambers. His friends and family called him Nick, or Nicky; bar patrons and Morgan knew him as Jarrod.

Nick's was strict on age and dress code. No one under thirty, men weren't allowed to wear hats or baseball caps, and no gym shoes or jogging suits. He wanted to attract a steady, but upscale clientele. Much like Morgan.

Nick shrugged his shoulders. He knew that if he waited any longer, he'd lose his nerve and not ask Morgan out. And he knew he couldn't stand her coming in his bar treating him like a buddy another night. He looked at the clock and decided to call Jackson.

"Ready for that can?" Nick laughed.

"Only if you are, old man." Jackson teased.

"Are you sure? I mean, you have been MIA a lot, lately," Nick asked.

"I know, but I'm free this morning. And I've got something to tell you."

"Oh? What is it?" Nick inquired.

"I'll tell you at the court. We'll meet at 31st since the weather is good today. How long you gonna take to get ready, old man?"

Nick laughed. "It's gonna take me fifteen minutes to dress and even less to lay you out!"

"Bet. See you at the court."

Nick laid back and thought about his boyhood friend and their ritual. Since they were teenagers, Nick and Jackson had played basketball nearly every Sunday morning. Yet, for the past several months, Jackson had begun backing out on their ritual—a little one on one, then a pick up game with court regulars, followed by some soul food at any local soul food spot, ending with any sports game on television. He then wondered what Jackson had to say. He hoped it wasn't another blind date. Tanya was more than enough to last him a lifetime.

He sniffed at that last thought. Would Morgan be too much for him to handle?. He hadn't a clue as to what her last name was, much less what she did for a living. He remembered she told him something about being in public relations, but outside of that, he didn't know her interests, her likes, anything outside of her favorite drink, Malibu Rum and Pineapple juice. That's all he knew. But it's time to change all that, he thought as he tossed the pillow across the room and got out of bed. He brushed his teeth, put on his basketball attire, a pair of red sweat pants and a long-sleeved white T-shirt, topped by a black leather coat. Nick hid his bloodshot eyes behind a pair of Ray Bans and placed a black White Sox hat over his closely cut hair. He climbed on his Harley for the short five-mile trek from his house to the beach.

"Hey, Jackson." Nick clasped his friend's hand as he pulled him into an embrace.

"What's happening, my brother?" Jackson replied.

"Not much." Nick began practicing his jump shot. He missed the first two, and then landed the following five. "Same ole thing. How's Yavette? That is her name, isn't it?"

"Man, you bad with names, but you got it right this time. And record this one, Nick. She's the one."

Nick felt a twinge of pain. Or was it jealously? He knew exactly what Jackson meant. He was going to ask her to marry him. So, this was what he wanted to tell him.

"Nick, my man, I've found her. The woman I want to marry."

"Yeah?" Nick took another shot. He landed it—all net.

Jackson swiped the ball out of the air. "Yeah."

The two fell into a quick game of one-on-one. Jackson pushed his stocky frame against Nick's and blocked shot after shot. After several blocks, Jackson stopped and held the ball under his arm.

"What gives, ole man?"

Nick swatted at the ball. "Hey, watch that old man crap."

Jackson put the ball down and placed his foot on top of it. "Seriously, you okay?"

"Yeah, why wouldn't I be?"

"No, I'm talking about what I just said. You know I want you to be my best man?"

"I kinda figured that. Who else would stand next to your nappy-headed ass?"

The pair laughed as the joke conjured up thoughts of high school, when people called them the Brillo Brothers because of their extremely coarse hair. When the short look became fashionable, Nick had begun cutting his close, making him appear bald from a distance.

"Hey, we're having a party. You know, getting our families and friends together to announce the engagement."

"You proposed already?"

"Yeah. Last night. I was scared, Nick, I really was. But, then I thought of my parents. Yavette is so much like my mother, it's scary."

"Do you love her?"

"More than I can say, man. More than I can say."

"Well, for the record, I like her, man. Really. She's a great woman. You're lucky."

"True that. But, hey, she's got a cousin."

"No, Jackson. No more blind dates. Okay?"

"But…"

"No!" Nick barked, signaling an end to their conversation.

The pair resumed their game. Several others joined them. For over three hours they played, as each man talked their own brand of garbage and attempted moves, twirls, in-the-air theatrics and slam-dunks. Twice, Nick had to pull Jackson out of somebody's face over a foul play. When they were finished, Nick's legs burned from the heavy workout. They sat on a nearby bench.

"Hey, I think you should let Yavette hook you up with her cousin."

Nick shook his head. "Man, you must have just lost your mind out there." He pointed to the basketball court. "Didn't I say no? I'm only a sucker once. That last one was a show stopper."

"Man, she's single, no kids and owns her own company."

"And?" Nick replied unimpressed as he rose from the bench.

"She's fine, man. Got a great head on her shoulders. And a nice body, if I dare say that."

Nick began to walk toward his motorcycle. "You thick up here, you know that."

He pointed to his head, and then straddled the cycle.

"Awright, man, don't say I didn't try. But you'd be a fool if you bypass a woman like Morgan so that she can keep going out on them crazy blind dates." Jackson began to walk away.

Nick stopped cold. He rose slowly from the bike. He wasn't sure he had he heard him right. He rushed over to Jackson. "What did you say her name is?" he almost whispered, his voice cagey.

"Morgan," Jackson replied. "Morgan Paige."

In all his wildest dreams, he couldn't have come up with this. His best friend's fiancée and Morgan were cousins. He had heard Morgan refer to a close relative a few times as Vettie, but he never gave much thought that it could have been short for Yavette.

Nick sat down hard on the grass as he shook his head. "Man, this is unbelievable."

"What?!" Jackson seemed alarmed.

"That's the sister who used to come into the bar nearly every Friday night before the renovations. I'm her favorite bartender."

"You know Morgan?"

"Yup." Nick smiled broadly. "Jackson, man, I almost asked her out about six months ago, but she only sees me as a bartender, and all we ever talked about were her dates from hell."

"Talk about a small world." Jackson sighed. "Does she know you own Nick's?"

Nick shook his head. He purposely let Morgan believe he was only a bartender. He wanted to see if she would be attracted to him. And up to that point she had treated him with warmth and kindness, but never any more than that.

"Wait. Did I hear you say something about blind dates?" Nick asked.

"Yeah. Yavette seems to think that Morgan should date more, so she has been hooking her up with these dudes. The first one, this past Friday, was a bust. I mean brotha man clowned! And poor Morgan, she agreed to three of them—so, she has two more to go."

Nick became excited. Maybe, just maybe, this was the right way to go. He'd finally get the opportunity to see Morgan outside of that bar. *You couldn't get any better than this!* He stood up, and then climbed back on his motorcycle.

"When is the party?"

"A month from this Saturday. But Yavette wants you two to meet before the engagement party."

"When?"

"About two weeks from now? On a Saturday. Yavette is having a little card party, and she's inviting the entire intended wedding party, excluding the parents. What do you think?"

"I think I wouldn't miss it for the world." Nick grinned and wondered if he could wait that long. Two weeks was a long time.

"You won't fake, will you?" Jackson eyed him.

"Naw man, I'm going to be there. But do me a favor? Don't tell her I'm her third blind date. Let me surprise her. And make sure you let Yavette know that *I'm* Morgan's final blind date."

Nick rode home with a grin so wide his face hurt. Never in his wildest dreams could this be happening. He would get the opportunity to show Morgan that even though she had had a few bad dates that he was the type of man she had been searching for. He wasn't arrogant. He saw himself as secure and self-assured. And besides, he had long given up being someone other than who he was just to please others Sheila had taught him that. Never try to be what you are not.

Nick dismounted and strolled up the walk to his house. He sang the song he had memorized and thanked his God for allowing him this one chance. A chance to make Morgan Paige all his. *Could he wait that long?* he wondered as he looked over the nights receipts from Nick's. He wasn't sure, but he knew one thing for sure, Morgan and those dates were over, it was time for her to meet Nicholas Jarrod Chambers, Jr.

CHAPTER 5

Yavette Ramsey strolled lazily along LaSalle Street as she headed to her office at Bell, Boyd & Lloyd. At 5'7", Yavette was statuesque, with her narrow waist and ample hips and medium bust line. It had taken her years to learn to accept her hour-glass shape. Growing up, she had wished she was built more like Morgan: toned, muscular legs, a tight behind that brothers use to say you could bounce a quarter off, a slight tummy and a perfect pair of "B" cups. Now, at the ripe age of thirty-two, she had slowly, but surely, accepted and learned to love the whole skin she was in. From the tops of shoulder length, sable hair, to the tips of her size nine feet, the road to self love and acceptance had been paved with naysayers: brothers who wanted you to look a certain way, dress a certain way, or eat a certain amount of food. And for many of the brothers she had wrongly chosen, it had hurt because she had fool-ishly changed into those things and found herself still empty, until she met Jackson.

In all her dating years, she had never met a man like Jackson Fisher. Six foot and the color of dark bronze, with a medium build and a smooth, perfectly round, bald head, Jackson had claimed her heart the moment she had laid in his arms and he informed her that he wasn't going anywhere. And since that admission almost a year ago, they had fought the pull of desire, while they sought emotional and spiritual fulfillment. In her heart, Yavette knew that once they made love, added that physical connect, that their souls would be in a never ending dance.

Yavette stopped at Caribou Coffee, and picked up her favorites: the house special with a hint of almond syrup and half a raisin bagel, no cream cheese. She continued on until she came to the four rows of brass and glass revolving doors. She had worked at the law firm for nearly five years, longer than any place she had ever been employed. As she walked, she smiled and said hello to the various brothers and sisters she passed along the way. And though she always smiled at the brothers, be they dressed in baggy attire or two-piece suits, her heart and mind belonged to one person—Jackson.

She had met Jackson at a charity function Morgan had dragged her to. She hadn't wanted to go. Her heart was in pieces from her most recent breakup, and she hadn't wanted Morgan to know. Her favorite cousin, who was more like a sister, seemed to be able to hold on to a date for longer than six months, whereas she seemed to flutter from man to man. She hadn't considered herself loose, but she did enjoy the solid feel of a man, the warm feeling when enveloped in a pair of large arms, the way a man's body moved in the heat of passion. But she also had come to recognize the game of chase and conquer and knew the signs of disinterest once she had been conquered.

So, when she met Jackson, she had no intentions of dating, much less involving herself in another physical, emotionally draining relationship. She wanted some time to herself, to heal her broken heart and to fall madly in love with herself. She had also sworn off physical relations—no matter what. Yet, when Jackson approached Yavette, she felt a strange charge shimmy up her bare arms and zap the right side of her head. She had looked around, sure that folks saw the bolt of lightening that struck her. When he extended his hand, then took hers in his, she stared into the deep brown pools of his eyes and saw a longing of sorts buried in them. Her heart softened, even though she wanted him to have a chink in his armor. It would be easier than letting the emotions swirling inside her come out and take over, giving her reason to flee.

Yet, for the rest of the evening, the two talked and danced. At the end of the charity affair, Yavette dropped off Morgan at home, and then met Jackson at 31st Street Beach, where they sat along the rocks and talked until the sun crested Lake Michigan. As the sun rose, Yavette had the distinct feeling that this would be the last man she dated.

"Good morning, Miss Ramsey. I have several messages for you."

Yavette smiled and retrieved her messages from the newest temp the firm had acquired. This one seemed to have staying power, seeing as how she wore tight blouses that stretched across large C cups and was as blonde as any white woman Yavette had ever seen. The managing partners, five men, one who was black, and a lone female, who was reported to be a lesbian, all seemed to be smitten with the latest find. Yavette guessed she'd be smitten too if you liked the blonde, stacked, yes-I-need-a-meal, though, pale look.

Yavette headed to her office, which was at the very end of the long hallway, to the left and over toward the corner. She didn't mind. When she was first assigned to the office, there had been an ugly brick building as her view. Well, the city had torn down the building and left behind a breathtaking view of LaSalle Street and the Chicago Board of Trade.

As she stepped over the threshold, she spotted Thomas as he walked toward his office. Yavette spun around and began to walk quickly down the adjoining hallway. She noticed that his steps seemed to pick up a little speed. Yavette did double time in her three-inch heels, her open blazer flapped behind her. She was on a mission.

She rounded another corner. Thomas turned and spied her gaining on him. He walked even faster, almost trotted as he tried to get away. He turned another corner. Yavette was closing in on him.

"Thomas," Yavette called out as he pushed open a door, then disappeared. Yavette followed. She gasped when she spotted two men standing at urinals. She hadn't realized that she had followed Thomas into the men's restroom. She apologized profusely as she backed out of the men's restroom. She wouldn't go there. On second thought, she would have, had Thomas lay a hand on Morgan, but he had just showed what an ass he really was, and Yavette was intent on telling him just how big a butt he had been to her cousin.

Yavette walked back toward her office. She would wait him out. Thomas always hung out with the boys on her side of the floor, which was where all the firm's expert litigants' offices were, hers included. She knew he'd have to come around eventually.

CUPID

Yavette removed her jacket, grabbed several tissues from the dispenser on her desk, and patted her brow. She sat down at her desk and opened the legal briefing she had left on Friday. She had another two weeks to prepare for a case in which a client was named in a wrongful death lawsuit. And though Yavette knew that the multi-million dollar industrial conglomerate was clearly innocent this time, they hadn't always been so. On many occasions, the firm had ridden to their rescue and bailed them out of countless situations. Yavette was relieved that she hadn't been asked to represent them on a case of questionable matter. True, she loved being an attorney, and prided herself on being one of the city's best torts litigants, but she didn't have the tough skin to defend those she felt were guilty and knew that one day this company would ask her to do just that. When that day came, she knew she would tender her resignation.

"Miss Ramsey. Call on line two. It's Jackson," the receptionist sang.

Yavette raised one eyebrow. *No, that dime-store blonde-haired woman didn't call my honey by his first name, and then sing it like he's in some video. That broad calls everyone by their surnames. Umm, gonna hafta straighten that out.* "Thank you, Miss Stewart."

"Hi, sweetie," Yavette sang into the receiver.

"How's my baby today?"

"Doing good. Missing you. How you feeling?"

"Better. I shouldn't have let you talk me into spending the night at my own place. You know I like waking up next to you."

Yavette smiled. "I know, but things have been," she paused and scrunched up her face. She wanted to be delicate with her words. "You know."

"Yeah, I know, baby. It has been getting harder and harder to sleep next to you and just hold you. We're going to have to do something about that sooner than later. How about we elope today?"

Yavette smiled. "My parents would have a fit. And you know Morgan's dad marries everyone—he's the family minister. Doesn't your mom want to see her baby boy get married?"

"You're right. But I'm telling you right now, I don't think I can wait a year. How about six months from now?"

"Ummm, now that sounds good. I think Morgan and I can pull it off in that time."

"Oh, speaking of Morgan, Nick is down for being her final date."

Yavette became quiet. She knew that Morgan was tired. She'd only been on one date thus far, and that had been a bust. Then she reluctantly agreed to go out with Tony. Maybe I should cancel both and let it go, she thought.

"Baby, what's wrong? Nick said yes. And besides, they know each other."

"They do? How?"

Yavette laughed as she listened to Jackson. There was no way this was happening, but then again, it saved her from trying to find the third blind date for Morgan.

"I know she goes to this bar, but she's never mentioned a guy named Nick. Oh, well. Anyway, I mentioned him to her, but she gave me the old evil eye. So, I didn't even get a chance to mention his name, much less anything else."

"Well, he wants to be her last date," Jackson said.

"Mr. Fisher, you have an urgent call holding." Yavette heard the voice through the receiver.

"Duty calls. I'll call you back. What are you doing for lunch?"

"Can't today. I'm working on a briefing. So I'll be right here reading."

"Okay, I'll call you later. Love you, baby."

"I love you, too."

Yavette placed the receiver on its base, then glanced over at the picture she and Jackson had taken a month after they had begun dating. In the year since, they had seemed to grow closer and closer, and she had never been more at ease, felt as safe, or as loved and wanted as Jackson made her feel. And they hadn't even made love. Yavette sighed. She hadn't told a soul—not even Morgan. She wasn't a virgin when she met Jackson, but she had also grown tired of giving her essence to yet another game-playing brother, which always left her empty and knowing that there was more out there, much more waiting for her other than empty words and broken promises. The night she met Jackson, he had admitted to her that he found himself embroiled in a series of spiritual lessons that had him practicing celibacy.

Yavette took this as a sign. She too had begun practicing celibacy and was a good six months into it when she met Jackson. She had never had a relationship that hadn't included sex, and knew it was easier to abstain when one wasn't in a relationship.

She looked at the picture again. She felt it. She knew it. And yes, she had accepted the love Jackson lavished upon her. Now, if she could just find Morgan a good date and get her married off, all would be well. Who knows, maybe Nick would be the man Morgan marries, the man to curl her toes. She snickered and thought about the look on Morgan's face the night she and their cousin talked about sexual pleasure. Morgan had looked lost.

Yavette looked up just in time to see Thomas slither by her office.

"Thomas Van Norton, I need to speak to you," Yavette called out as she rose from her seat, her hands placed on her full hips. No one plays games with them—no one!

Morgan sat at her cherry wood desk in her office and poured over several stacks of papers. The highly glossed top gleamed as she shuffled papers and books back and forth. She hated Monday mornings, prying over reports, answering clients' phone calls following their weekend forays, and playing catch-up on industry news. She looked at the clock. It read seven A.M. She then spied the small leather couch at the other end of the office. What she really wanted to do was to lie down and catch a few winks before Tina, her assistant, walked in. But she knew better. She knew that the reasons for her coming in so early on Mondays was so that she could be on top of her game by nine. And being on top of her game had paid off in the form of six figures, which allowed her to finally bask in the glory of her success. Her thoughts raced to Friday's events and her visit from Yavette on Saturday.

The pair had sat up all night talking just like they had when they were teenagers. After Yavette left the following day, Tony had called her cell number. Morgan didn't even want know why Yavette gave him her cell number. Had she given him every number she owned?

Yet, she had been surprised at the ease with which they talked, their conversation filtered in and out of current events, sports and even marriage. At the end of their hour-long conversation, they agreed to meet Friday.

Morgan thought of her upcoming date with Lawrence. They had agreed meet this coming Wednesday, after work, at the TGI Friday's downtown. He was her secret. And she had never kept secrets from the one woman who was more like a sister than a first cousin. In some ways, Morgan felt bad for not telling Yavette about her upcoming date with a man she met on the Internet, but just the same, she also was tired of being alone. No, she wasn't lonely—that was a different kind of feeling all together—she liked her company and could spend hours milling around her condo with nothing in particular planned. Since her divorce, Morgan had become even less regimented and allowed herself to be idle when needed. No, she was alone with no one special to cuddle up to on Chicago's cold nights or hold hands with during its beautiful summer days. But then again, Morgan had chosen to be alone. Now she longed to have a special someone in her life.

Morgan thought about Yavette. She liked Jackson for Yavette—liked how he made her feel loved and special—like she was the only woman in the whole world. Then her thoughts trailed to Thomas. In spite of it all, she had to laugh at the incident at the restaurant.

Morgan removed several papers from her leather briefcase. Her fingers caught on the flier from Nick's Sports Bar and Grille. She smiled warmly, then remembered that the bar now hosted several theme nights. Tonight was "Throw Back to the Funky 80's Night." Tuesday was "Soul Food Night," Wednesday was "Bid Whist" and Thursday, the day Mr. Johnson had mentioned, was "Stepper's Night."

Morgan looked at her watch. Her assistant Tina would be waltzing through the door with two muffins—a banana nut for Morgan and a blueberry for herself—and coffee. She smiled when she heard Tina's soothing voice as she sung. She thought Tina had a great voice. The one time she had asked her why she hadn't pursued a singing career, Tina's eyes glazed over with sadness, and she responded with a shrug.

"Mornin', Boss Lady. How was your weekend?" Tina poked her head around the open door.

"Just fine, Tina. And yours?"

"Great." Tina stepped into the office. She pulled the muffins from the bag, placed them on a napkin, followed by two cups of coffee on the round, cherry wood table that sat at the far end of the large office. Morgan rose and sat at one of the four matching chairs. She smiled at Tina; then bowed her head slightly to sip the hot liquid. She watched Tina as she sat across from her and began her normal ritual of catching Morgan up on all the latest happenings, both within the sports world and with their clients. Morgan nodded and watched Tina, her small facial features, highlighted by the short, curly Afro, seemed to beam.

Tina had been with Morgan since the beginning, when things had been rough and she hadn't had enough money to properly pay either one of them. But Tina had stuck in there and was now Morgan's executive assistant, with a great salary and annual bonus.

"What's on the plate for today?" Morgan drained the last of her coffee, then popped the last morsel of muffin into her mouth.

"Too much. You've got that meeting with the prospective client. And if you've read the papers, our boy is at it again."

Morgan sighed. The "boy" Tina referred to was one of her first clients, William Johnson, the explosive tight end for the Tennessee Titans. In four years, Morgan had taken William, or Willie as he liked to be called, from virtual obscurity to a household name. But there was just one problem—Willie loved women. Too much. No matter the size, shape or color, he hadn't met a woman he didn't like.

"What did our golden child do now?" Morgan asked.

"Wait till you see this," Tina said as she left the office. She returned moments later and tossed several newspapers on the table.

Morgan closed her eyes and inhaled deeply. She opened her eyes and began to read the various headlines. "Willie Johnson Fathers Again," screamed one headline from a dime-store rag. "Willie Strikes a Third Time," the Chicago Sun-Times sports page blared. Morgan threw the papers to the floor.

"All the rest of the papers covered the story. He hasn't called you?"

Morgan huffed and raked her fingers through her twists. "You know he didn't." She rose and picked up the phone at the corner of her desk. She dragged the entire contraption to the opposite side of the room and stood in front of the floor to ceiling window. She dialed his private line.

After four rings, a groggy Willie answered, "Speak to Big Daddy."

"William Johnson, what's going on with you?" Morgan spoke evenly, though she wanted to scream and then create a campaign for birth control, with him as the poster boy.

"Aw, baby girl, they just hatin' on a brotha."

"Okay, maybe so, but are the stories true? It's in all the papers here. And I'm sure they're in every paper there." Morgan turned as Tina handed her several pages from the UPI wire service. Sure enough, just about every newspaper outlet across America covered his latest paternal escapade.

"Naw, I used a rubber with that girl."

"Well, seems as if the rubber broke. I'll see you tomorrow after practice. I'll fly out first thing. Don't talk to anyone until I get there. Hear me? I'll call the man."

They both chuckled at the pet name they had given Harlen Schneider, the attorney Morgan had hired to represent her more high maintenance clients, ones just like Willie. She would have Harlen look into the background of Willie's latest conquest. She needed to know all about the female leveling charges against her favorite client.

For three hours, Morgan and Tina created a public relations coup to stave off any further damage the horrid story could create, which included a four o'clock press conference in Nashville, right after practice.

By the time lunch came and went, Morgan was exhausted with at least another six hours to go.

"Ms. Paige, Mr. Duffy is here," Tina spoke professionally into the intercom.

"Please send him in."

Morgan rose to meet her next potential client, who was looking to score big off the almighty black dollar. She liked these types. It was a chance for her to create a marketing and public relations schematic that would cast her people in a more positive light.

She smiled warmly as Mr. Duffy stepped into her office and offered his hand. Morgan shook his hand, and then instructed him to sit in one of the chairs at the round table.

During their meeting, she had watched Mr. Duffy with detached amusement as he grappled with a way to convey to her his desire to market his product to Black America. She could see he wasn't entirely comfortable, she sensed this was his first voyage into the deep pockets of Black America, even though Mr. Duffy had been in business for over forty years.

In two hours, Morgan had outlined several ideas and produced marketing data to substantiate her proposal. She ended with a handshake and a signature on the dotted line to create and execute a plan to market high-end time shares to African-Americans.

CHAPTER 6

Nick stepped from his SUV and headed into the club. He spoke to the few regulars who dotted the bar and headed to his office. He thought of his regulars. The ones who had sustained Nick's before he purchased it, and nodded to himself. These were the ones who kept the place going, allowed it to remain solvent even during the six months they were closed for renovations. They had promised to always patronize Nick's, and they hadn't let him down. Nick peered out of the square, one-way mirror on the door of the office. He thought of Morgan and wondered, if indeed she would return before Friday.

He moved from the door and sat behind the desk. He looked at the stack of receipts and invoices, picked up a pen and began to meticulously go over the various documents that needed his immediate attention. His MBA came in handy. This, he reasoned, had prepared him to run a successful business, even though that business dealt in the serving of what many considered sin—liquor.

After countless hours of pouring over papers, greeting distributors and stocking shelves, Nick took several moments to prepare himself for the night's events. He checked the DJ's play list. He laughed as he looked down the list and saw several of his favorites. "Smart man," he mumbled when he spotted the song "I Want You for Myself," by George Duke. The list contained songs he had partied hard to during the funk age of the 80s.

"Nick."

He heard his name and looked up to see his brother Nehemiah come through the door.

"What's up? How you doing?"

Nehemiah sat down on the small, black leather love seat along the far wall of the office. At least 6'4", Nehemiah stretched out his long legs in front of him and crossed his arms across his large chest. "Hey, I've been better. But what can I say? I knew. I just chose to ignore it." He rubbed his large hands across his bearded face. "Knew it from day go."

Where Nick looked like their father and David looked like their mother, Nehemiah had a mix of both—his smooth cocoa skin was a mix of their mother's caramel complexion and their father's chocolate one. His face was round, like their mother's, his broad nose their father's, and his slightly slanted, light brown eyes, their mother's. As he watched his brother struggle with the words bubbling at the surface, Nick could see that Nehemiah's pride was more stung than hurt.

"Don't beat yourself up over it." Nick leaned across the desk. "We've all been somebody's fool."

Nick watched Nehemiah wince at the words he'd just spoken. "Anyway, that's now water under the bridge. What's going on around here today?"

Nick let the conversation change. He didn't want to press the issue with Nehemiah. He'd allow his brother to speak on it as he needed to. "I'm just getting ready for tonight. Last week I had to put folks out. They wanted to stay past 2 A.M., And you know the liquor commissioner ain't having that," Nick responded.

"I hear ya. Well, what do you need me to do?"

Nick wanted to tell his brother to go home and get some rest, but he also knew that Nehemiah needed something to do. Especially since he would never be able to hold a job. Nehemiah had been in a near-fatal car accident four years ago that left him in a coma for nearly a month with countless contusions, abrasions and broken bones in his upper body and arms. Though he had sued the trucking company and walked away with a few million dollars, Nehemiah had only partial use of his right arm and hand, his writing hand, and little to no use of his left. But God had protected him, and Nehemiah hadn't lost his gentle, gregarious nature.

"How about you come up with something, a contest with a five-hundred-dollar pot, to surround tonight's theme?" Nick asked.

Nehemiah smiled. "Yeah, like a bump contest."

Nick laughed. "No, that was the 70s. This is an 80's funk party. What was hot then?"

Nehemiah titled his head to the side. "Hot pants."

The pair fell out in laughter. After several minutes of raucous laughter, they sobered. Nick spoke first. "You crazy. But you may have something there. Halloween's in a couple of weeks. Work on a theme surrounding the 70's. I'm talking platform shoes, Afro wigs, and the whole nine."

"Mr. Johnson will win hands down. He still thinks green and orange suits with matching shoes and hats are the rage." Nehemiah stood. "I'll get started. We'll have some type of dance contest. The whop, the funk, something. Whatever, it'll be the bomb, 'cause you're gonna have to pay to keep folks outta here."

Nick stood and rounded the desk. He put his arms around his brother's neck and hugged him tightly.

"Thanks, Nicky." Nehemiah used his boyhood nickname, then left the office.

Nick watched his retreat. He hung his head and thought of what a fool he had been for Sheila. "Yeah, that's water under the bridge, too." He squared his shoulders and left the office to finish the preparations for the night's event.

Morgan stretched her body. From the points of her toes, clad in black tights, to her fingers, she raised her arms above her head. She looked at the flier from Nick's. She could go for some 80's music.

"Tina," Morgan called toward the outer office as she fished under the desk for her high-heeled boots. "Am I all set to leave for Nashville in the morning?"

Tina walked over to the desk and handed her the boarding pass, Willie's client file and a plastic folder containing a stack of press releases. "Sure are, Boss Lady. Your flight leaves at 9:30 and arrives in

Nashville at 11. I've booked you a rental. The press conference is after practice, then you have a 7 P.M. dinner with a potential client, courtesy of Willie. He called while you were in your meeting. You know he feels bad."

"Hell, he should." Morgan walked around her office, pulling sheets and files from various shelves and drawers. Her hands waved in the air as she spoke. "That Nike deal just landed on the table." Morgan paused, looked under a stack of paper. She shook her head before she continued. "I'm afraid to call them. It took me months to sell them on even thinking about giving him an endorsement deal. I'm going to strangle him."

"Well, you may want to just pat our child on the wrist."

Morgan stopped and looked at Tina, her right eyebrow raised. "Why?"

"Guess who Willie set you up with?"

Morgan cringed and her head spun. She had only agreed to three. Three! No! No more blind dates!

"Keith Bullock."

Morgan sighed. Her mind stopped spinning and her pulse regulated. Keith Bullock was one of the Titan's most respected players— both on the field and off. She knew that if she were able to add Bullock, an outside linebacker with both talent and speed, it would make Paige PR a major player in the male-dominated world of sports. In addition, having Bullock as a client would give her the opportunity to create a marketing/public relations plan around the defensive player. Most companies wanted either a quarterback or running backs and wide receivers. They weren't really interested in the beefy backs that helped the team score or kept their opponent from scoring.

"I'll kiss Willie first, then I'll slap him upside his head. That Nike deal is still in jeopardy." Morgan paused. "So, wait." She sat down. "I won't be back until late. Did you schedule me to return Wednesday morning?"

"Yes, I did. Are you okay with that?" she asked. "I knew you'd be okay with meeting with Mr. Bullock. Oh, and he called to confirm."

"I'm good. Don't forget to put together a packet for Mr. Bullock." Morgan looked up at Tina and smiled. She'd be truly lost without her.

Morgan would be back in time to go on her date with LawMann, aka Lawrence on Wednesday night. She wondered was it the right thing to do, even though they had talked on the phone several times over the past two months and had taken months before that online before they mutually agreed to meet. He had sent her a picture of himself, albeit it was a little grainy. She could make out his light complexion and his muscular frame. Thinking of muscular, she thought about Jarrod, then smiled.

"Okay, Boss Lady. What are you thinking about? I haven't seen that look on your face since Willie brought his cousins to your birthday party."

Morgan rolled her eyes heavenward and waved an imaginary fan across her face. She had held the party for her birthday as well as to celebrate Paige's fifth year in business. Held at the elegant Palmer House, over 250 people attended—only a fraction was clients. But all the women in the place, young and old, married or single, stopped when Willie, no ugly brother himself, walked through the door flanked by four of the most gorgeous brothers any of them had laid eyes on. Even Morgan swooned at the complete beauty of the brothers. They created even more of a stir when they all came to stop in front of Morgan, who'd been swept up into Willie's massive arms right before he presented her with a woman's Rolex watch as a birthday gift. As he sat her on her feet, Willie introduced Morgan to his cousins from Alabama, all incredibly tall, incredibly built and fantastically fine. The night had been one to remember, with Morgan dancing with each cousin. And though two of the cousins, Bobby Joe and Joe Willie, wanted her phone number, she hadn't obliged—her feelings from the finality of the divorce, which was the same week as her birthday, were still too raw for her. Of course, Yavette had said she was crazy, but Morgan knew she did not want to get involved in a relationship at the time.

Morgan laughed and shook her head. "Them boys were something else. Made quite a stir with the women, but I'm okay. I've got to call my parents, though, and then let's wrap up for the night. I've got a stop to make."

Morgan had spoken with her parents, informing them that she was heading to Nashville and returning to Chicago on Wednesday morning. She had spoken with her mother, Norma, followed by her father, Ishmael, who had said a prayer and bade her a safe trip. As Morgan hung up, she thought about Jarrod and the bar. Her father would like Jarrod, but would dismiss him the moment he found out that he worked at a bar. Morgan's father had always blamed his father's ill behavior or liquor. And though Grandpa Mack was ninety years old and doing well, her father hadn't quite gotten over the times Grandpa Mack had come home in a nasty, drunken rage.

For three additional hours, Morgan and Tina worked on the press materials, followed by the short presentation for Mr. Bullock before Morgan announced that it was time to quit.

As Morgan prepared to leave her office, Tina handed Morgan her full-length, black leather coat and black briefcase as Morgan stepped into her ankle boots. Tina looked over Morgan's desk. She wanted to be sure that Morgan hadn't left anything behind. "Hey, what's this?" Tina held up the flier. "Nick's Sports Bar and Grille. Where the mature meet and mingle." Tina looked at Morgan. "Sounds nice. Have you been?"

Morgan slid into her coat. "Yes, I went Friday night to the grand reopening. It was a nice spot before, but it's even nicer now. The renovations really added a special touch to the bar. The drinks are reasonable, and they have a great menu."

"I'm going to have to check this joint out."

"You should do that. I had a great time."

"Are you going tonight? It's 80's funk night."

She looked up at Tina and read the mischief in her eyes. "Why? You want to go with me?"

"You mind?"

"No, not at all. I'm going to stop and get my nails done. I should get there by eight."

"Bet. I'll meet you at the spot. Who knows, I may find my prince charming there."

Morgan laughed and thought about Jarrod. "You just may. Okay, lock up, and I'll see you at eight."

Manicure complete, Morgan headed to Nick's and hoped that Jarrod would be there. She had to admit that one of the reasons she wanted to return to the bar was to see Jarrod. Maybe this time whatever he had to say he'd say it. Or maybe, just once in her life, she'd ask a man out—she'd ask Jarrod out for a date. They could go out to dinner, maybe walk along Michigan Avenue hand in hand. She then thought about his face, that cute, chocolate chip complexion with those deep, sexy dimples. *Naw, a brother that good looking has to have a girlfriend. No way can he be like me, spending nights alone with two scrappy animals and a pint of ice cream.*

She rolled along the street, the face of the man she was crazy about firmly implanted in her mind.

"Welcome back to Nick's, Miss Morgan."

Morgan looked up and smiled at the bouncer who had introduced himself as Craig. "Why thank you, Craig. I told you I'd be back."

He smiled as Morgan handed her car key to the valet, then walked beside the beefy bouncer. He opened the door for her. "Have a great night and thank you for returning to Nick's."

Morgan nodded her head and entered the bar. Her eyes adjusted as her head began to bob to the heavy beat of Parliament's "Flash Light." Instinctively her body began to shimmy to the beat, the sound of Bootsy Collins's thunderous bass seemed to rattle all of the glasses that lined the bar's shelves. She began to do a dance called the Spank as Tina shimmered over to her in a pair of three inch pumps, her fitted black leather mini skirt moved with her, the matching blazer gave a peek of a red bustier, which boasted a tasteful amount of cleavage. Her face lit up as she broke into her own rendition of the dance called the Errol Flynn.

"Girl, this joint is live. And they gots some fine brothers waiting these tables."

Morgan laughed as Tina continued to dance as she made her way over to a table in the Sports Arena. Tina flopped down into the chair. "They have been jamming since I got here. The bartender said that once they start the dance contest that the roof will certainly raise."

Morgan removed her coat and sat down. She looked around the place and frowned slightly when she didn't spot Jarrod. To her, he was the main attraction. She picked up the menu from the table.

"What can I get you ladies this evening?"

Morgan smiled as her eyes trailed up the large hands holding the pad, but held no pen. She tried to hide her obvious disappointment when her eyes rested on the tall brother who favored Jarrod, but was not him. "I'll take…"

"Thanks, man. I'll take care of them."

"Jarrod."

"Hey, Morgan," he greeted her. "How are you on this beautiful night?"

She smiled up at him as his deep dimples came into view with the summoning of his warm smile. She felt the beads of water forming on her forehead and upper lip. *Dang!* He handed her a napkin.

"It is kinda warm in here," he said and smiled.

She looked in his eyes and saw the innocence in them. He hadn't a clue as to what his voice did to her, the effect his presence elicited, and no man had ever elicited this type of reaction. *If he only knew.* She inhaled deeply as her pulse began to run away, pounding furiously at her pressure points. "That it is. But, I'm good. And you?"

"Better. Definitely much better," he beamed at her and pulled a seat out and sat down. "I've got a few moments. How've you been, really?" Morgan blushed as she looked at him, his cologne swirling around her, his eyes drawing her into a hypnotic spell. If she didn't know any better, she'd swear that Jarrod was coming on to her. "I wasn't sure I'd see you again. I really should have gotten your number that night, but I was a little slow."

Morgan blinked several times. "Are you faster now?"

He threw his head back and laughed heartily. "Much." He looked into her eyes and smiled at her. "Now, I guess I should do some work. Would you like the usual?"

She nodded, her voice stuck. And as if they had just noticed, Morgan's eyes rolled to rest on Tina. Jarrod followed suit.

"My apologies." He faced Tina. "I know what she's having. What will you have?"

"I'll take a glass of Merlot."

"I'll be right back with your drinks. See anything on the menu?"

Morgan looked up at Jarrod then to the menu. She attempted to study the menu. She raised her eyes to see Tina peering at her. Morgan squinted. "Umm, how about the strip steak sandwich, well done, with a side of seasoned fries?" She looked up at Jarrod and noticed that his smile, the sexy glint in his eyes, remained fixed on her.

Tina cleared her throat. "And I'll take the shrimp and chips, side salad and garlic bread."

"Will do. Be right back."

"And how about that fine brother on a plate?" Tina snickered once Jarrod left their table. Morgan looked at her and noticed the cat-o-mouse expression on her face.

"What?"

"Hi, Jarrod. Hi, Morgan," Tina mimicked in a sing-song voice. "No wonder you've come back here. I'd come back, too."

"You don't know what you're talking about."

"Sure, Boss Lady, tell me anything."

Nick appeared just as Morgan was about to protest Tina's words.

"Here ya go. And your food will be up shortly." He placed square coasters on the table, followed by their drinks. "Be back." He left quickly. Morgan watched him walk away. His black jeans hugged his rear. She inhaled deeply.

"Umph. Somebody's got it bad."

Morgan waved her hand at Tina in a motion of dismissal.

"Well, here's my girl." Mr. Johnson pulled up a chair and sat down. He stretched out his hand to Tina. "I know her, but I don't know you. My name is Duke. And lovely lady, you are?"

Tina smiled warmly and extended her hand. She giggled as Mr. Johnson kissed the back of her proffered hand. "Tina."

"Well, Tina, it's a pleasure to meet you. Hey, Miss Morgan, how are you today?"

"Doing good, Mr. Johnson, and you?"

"Much better now that I have not only one, but two very beautiful seat mates." He raised his hand above his head. Tina and Morgan followed his line of vision and watched as the taller version of Jarrod approached their table.

"Hey, Nehemiah. I'll take a Jack with water back."

"Sure thing, Mr. Johnson. Good to see you." Nehemiah nodded.

"Same here. Is your father coming tonight?"

"Naw, he said he may come Thursday."

"I'll call him. Thanks."

Once their food arrived, Morgan and Tina sat back and enjoyed their respective meals, which were interspersed with tales from Mr. Johnson and the previous owner. The trio had laughed as he told the story after story. His smooth, nutmeg brown face made animated gestures at all the right junctures in his tales.

"All right ladies and gentlemen. Time to get your funk on. Get a partner. Nick's Sports Bar and Grille is proud to announce the 80's funk dance contest. Five hundred dollars will go to the best dancer of the Wop, the Puppet, Punk—all those dances that made the 80's funky!"

Mr. Johnson laughed when Morgan looked at him. "No way, Miss Morgan. I'm seventy-four years old and the only dancing I do is a little bob and step. The 80's are way outta my league."

Morgan blinked. She had guessed he was in his early sixties. She had no idea that he was older than her own father.

"Okay, I'll let you off the hook this time. But next time."

"Thank you, Miss Morgan." He nodded his head.

She glanced around the bar. She spotted Jarrod behind the bar. He smiled at her. She returned the gesture, and then noticed a caramel-colored brother standing alone, bobbing his head to the intro of Funkadelic's "One Nation Under A Grove."

"Time to win that money," Tina announced as she stood and walked over to Nehemiah, who was standing near the DJ's booth. She put her hand out to him. And when he didn't raise his hand, she grabbed him by his right forearm and dragged him onto the dance floor. Morgan laughed as Tina began to do the Spank, followed by the infamous Penicillin Drop, which was a dance that was actually from the late 70's. Morgan looked back toward Jarrod. She frowned inside when she didn't spot him. She shrugged her shoulders and watched as the caramel brother in a matching denim outfit strolled over to her.

"Want to try?" he asked. Morgan nodded her head and rose from her seat.

The heavy bass pumped from the speakers, and Morgan began to dance, her twists moved with her when she shook her head and raised her hand over her head. She danced to one song after the next as one of the servers wove in and out of the crowd of dancers and tapped individuals on the shoulder, indicating that they were to have a seat. Morgan's dance partner had been tapped, as had Tina, which left she and Nehemiah.

As the next song mixed in, they began to do the Wop, then the Pop, as their heads bobbed up and down and their legs worked in sync. Morgan began to do the Puppet, her feet moving effortless under her.

She found herself laughing out loud. She hadn't had this much fun in a long time. As the next song started, she upped the stakes and began to do an old punk funk move. She shimmed up to her dance partner and held him by the waist as she moved her hips to and fro.

CUPID

Nick swallowed hard as he watched his brother and Morgan from the DJ's booth. She was dressed in form fitting jeans, a black Turtleneck and high-heeled black boots. He watched the wicked sway of her hips and the way her round behind jutted out perfectly. The vision stirred him to the very core of that which made him man. He tried to swallow past what felt like a sand storm raging in the middle of his throat.

"Nick, she's smokin' Nehemiah!" the DJ said as he spun in a house tune. "Glad you ain't my brother."

He could only nod as he continued to watch Morgan begin a freestyle dance that was indigenous to the punk funk era of the eighties.

On the dance floor, Nehemiah tried to hold his own as he watched his dance partner simply out dance him. He looked over his shoulder to the DJ booth and signaled for the end of this contest. Morgan had won, hands down.

"Ladies and gentlemen, we have a winner. Young lady, come claim your prize."

Morgan squealed in delight and rushed to the booth. She stopped short when Jarrod handed her five, crisp one hundred dollar bills.

"Let's give Morgan a hand," the DJ spoke into the microphone.

Morgan turned and bowed demurely to the clapping crowd, then faced Jarrod.

"Morgan, I didn't know you could dance like that. As a matter of fact, I don't know much about you. But I know one thing."

She smiled up at him. "What?"

He titled his head to the side, his face coming closer to hers. She stared into his eyes and waited, anticipation made her pulse run rapid.

"You put a hurtin' on my brother." He smiled. "He's gonna have to take a long soak to recover from that spanking. Not to mention his reputation."

"I didn't know that was your brother." She thought about the familiar resemblance. She watched as he nodded, his eyes rested on her lips. She did likewise and noted smooth fullness of his as he licked them. Her palms began to sweat as he stepped even closer, close enough that she could see the strobe lights dance off his irises.

"Nick, call on line one," a female voice came out over the music.

"Yeah, he's my older brother." He stood over Morgan, his gazed fixed. As the slow song came out over the speakers, he wanted to pull her into his arms, close to his body, and sway with her to the sensuous tune of the Isley Brothers "Make Me Say it Again."

For awkward moments, the pair stood and watched each other.

"Nick, call on line one," the voice repeated again.

"Got a bar to tend to. Please stay and continue to enjoy your evening," Jarrod said as he reluctantly walked away from her.

Morgan folded the now damp money and placed the bills in her back pocket. She walked over to the table.

"Too bad he couldn't dance," Tina said as Morgan sat down.

Yeah, too bad, Morgan thought as she sipped her drink.

"Excuse me," Nehemiah appeared at their table. "Is there anything else you'd ladies like this evening?"

Tina batted her eyes, her lashes touching the tops of her high cheekbones. "Umm, I think I'd like another glass of Merlot."

"Coming right up. And you? The woman who spanked me unmercifully on that dance floor."

Morgan batted her eyes at him. "No. Not me. But if you'll forgive me and bring me a ginger ale, I'll be most grateful."

"And I'll be most grateful if you don't spank me like that again. I'm in pain, sistah." He smiled, then added, "I'll be right back with y'all's drinks. Don't go away," Nehemiah said as he looked at Tina.

"Somebody's interested."

Tina smiled. "He's good looking. He looks like Jarrod."

"Jarrod said they're brothers."

"Umph. They're both fine, but seeing as how Jarrod has the eyes for you, I'll take Nehemiah."

The pair laughed. Throughout the night, several men asked them to dance. Both happily obliged. And each time Morgan rose to dance, she had spied Jarrod as he stood off to the side and watched her. *If only,* she sighed.

Close to midnight, Morgan decided to call it a night. She had to pack for her flight in the morning.

As she and Tina headed to the entrance, Morgan looked around, her eyes searched for Jarrod among the countless faces in the bar. When she spotted him, she smirked. He was talking to two women sitting at the bar. *Why should I care that they're sitting in the very space I used to occupy?* She stole one last glance in their direction, squared her shoulders, and then continued out of the bar. She stopped when Mr. Johnson came up behind her and tapped her on the shoulder.

"Don't forget about Thursday night. That's steppers night, and I'll need a dance partner."

"I'll see, Mr. Johnson."

"Good enough. Night-night, Miss Morgan and Miss Tina."

"Good night, Mr. Johnson." Morgan smiled and stepped forward when she saw her car being driven by the valet. "Tina, I'll call you once I land."

"Sounds good, Boss Lady."

Morgan walked toward her car. She turned around to search for Tina. She smiled when she spotted Tina as she stood next to Nehemiah. Tina's face beamed as she looked up into his tanned cocoa colored one.

Morgan called out to Tina and waved as she settled behind the wheel of her car. As she began to pull away from the curb, she looked toward the entrance. She spotted Jarrod standing on the sidewalk near the doorway, his arms folded across his broad chest. She turned her head and headed into the late night traffic.

CHAPTER 7

Tina walked into her loft apartment just as the sun rose. She stretched as she sat on the cushion in the large bay window looking over the quiet streets of her Bronzeville community. She smiled as she thought of the long, deep conversations she and Nehemiah shared after Morgan left. She had seen him when she first arrived and noted the deep sadness in his light eyes, so like his brother's. And when he looked at her, she saw the longing in his eyes, the sadness that crept there and seemed to take up residence, made her want to reach out and sooth the furrow from his brows, kiss the sadness away from his face.

She was surprised when he stepped to her at the end of the night. She sat with him and his brother, Jarrod, as they cleaned up the bar, washing glasses, wiped down the bar and swept up. Their conversation remained light, focusing on all the surface stuff, the where'd you go to college, where'd you grow up. Once the brothers were finished, she watched as Jarrod jumped on his motorcycle, leaving them standing outside of the bar.

For over two hours they stood and talked, their words flowed effortlessly as the truth flowed between and around them, swallowing them up into a world of comfort. Neither had ever experienced anything like it—had never ever wanted to disclose so much in so little time—until now. The feelings to do so was inexplicable and literally caught both of them by surprised.

For Tina, she had loved, unconditionally, the same man for almost a decade. And each year she had hoped—had hoped she was good enough for him to marry—and each year he had a different excuse. Finally, Tina looked at herself in the mirror, took stock of what she brought to her own table, dropped forty pounds, met Morgan and left the man she'd placed all her dreams and love on. For the past five years, she hadn't wanted to date seriously. Oh she went out to dinner, attended plays with a select few men, but she hadn't bothered to give any her heart. And had only shared her body with one, during a real weak moment when her body overrode her mind.

When she mentioned going to Nick's, she hadn't expected to meet anyone that would make her take a second glance, but there was something in Nehemiah's gaze, the sadness in his eyes. She'd hoped that he didn't suffer from a broken heart and wasn't on the rebound.

Once they started talking, she'd got the impression that he was searching for something more—looking for someone to tell him all was well—that he had the capacity to still love. She'd been shocked at the simple, but blunt candor in which he discussed his pending divorce, the woman he'd chose to marry and his desire to move past the physical.

Tina had tried to inject humor in the conversation in an attempt to deflect the seriousness the conversation was traveling in. She wanted to believe—wanted to have his words, whispered on a wish, to be true. In the end, she'd looked up into his eyes, dark from the night, nodded her head and stepped from his Volvo.

She stretched and shook her head. She knew that she needed to grab at least a couple of hours of sleep before she had to head into the office. And with Morgan out of town, she knew she had to be on her toes and ready for anything that may come her way. Morgan had left her in charge.

As she lay across her bed, she said a silent prayer that, for once, she'd be able to believe, to be able to give herself freely, shedding the cloak of fear and apprehension. Once sleep claimed her, she felt a warmth blanket her, and she smiled as she drifted off.

Morgan stepped from the plane and watched as a woman ran into the arms of a man. He picked her up and held her close, then closed his eyes as she bent her head down to capture his lips.

As she walked around them, she smiled, silently wishing that there was someone to greet her like that, make her feel a part of another. After last night, the tone in Jarrod's voice, the way he set his stare upon her, Morgan knew that she could no longer pretend that she wasn't interested.

She knew nothing about chasing after men, taking that first step and asking a man out. Her mother had always told her that a proper woman never asked a man out or made it obvious that she was interested—that it's a man's job to ask a woman for a date. Well, she thought, if she waited for Jarrod, she may never get the chance. But before all of that, her getting up enough nerve to ask him out, she needed to tell him what she really did for a living, that her personal salary last year reached six figures. She didn't want him to run, didn't want the fact that he tended bar and she ran her own company to stand in their way, but she also had heard of men who had issues with women making more than them, that they couldn't handle it.

Morgan blinked her eyes. Her last thought hurt. She found herself liking Jarrod, and didn't want to believe that his ego would dictate that he had to make more than her in order to even consider going out with her.

She thought about her ex-husband, Michael. He hadn't been too keen on her opening her own business, much less making more money than he did. She'd been so in love with Michael, she'd never thought that they would just fall out of love, him first then finally Morgan. That was always deep to her—how two people so in love as they had been could just unceremoniously fall out of love. *How does one do that? Was the love real in the first place? Or, did we want to be so in love we overlooked the obvious?* Morgan shook her head. The answers to her questions always left her slightly melancholy. She just didn't want that type of relationship again—didn't want to feel that type of pain ever again.

Her thoughts tumbled until they rested on Jarrod for the umpteenth time that day.

To her, money didn't matter. She wanted a man who would stand by her side when things were good, have her back when she needed to lean, and stand in front of her when she needed protecting. Yet there was something about Jarrod that didn't indicate his ego led him.

Her steps quickened as she dragged her carry-on behind her and headed to the area that would take her to retrieve her rental car, then on to the coliseum where the Titans practiced and played.

For over an hour she watched as the Titans went through drills and executed plays. Morgan smiled at the sight of Willie as he blocked a receiver, which caused a fumble, and he ran into the end zone for a touch down. She laughed aloud as Willie began an old two-step. His large frame shimmied to and fro. Her eyes caught site of several new players, mostly rookies, as they went about their drills. One rookie in particular, Raheem Mohammed, caught her attention. She knew from the sports rags that Raheem had been a first round draft pick and had been courted by every major agent and PR firm known to the sports world. Morgan hadn't even thought of approaching the twenty-two-year-old running back, opting to sit back and see who he signed to represent him, and the types of publicity and endorsement deals he'd obtain.

At the end of practice, she waited in the media room, where she'd stand with Willie as he answered questions surrounding his latest escapade. It wouldn't be so bad if Willie hadn't already sired three children with two different women, having elected to forgo marrying either. After the birth of his third child, Willie Junior, three years ago, Willie swore he'd be more discerning and more cautious in his personal dealings with women.

Morgan shook her head. She heard Willie before she saw him, andbraced herself for his signature bear hug.

"There's mah girl," Willie shouted, and rushed over to Morgan, picking her up and hugging her close to his barrel chest. Morgan didn't dare squirm. She knew that Willie would tighten his grip versus loosening it. She rode out the vice-like, yet loving, hug.

"You ready?" she asked him as he placed her on her feet.

"'Bout as ready as I'm ever going to be. But I want to talk to you first." Willie's brown eyes looked into Morgan's. "I need to tell you something."

Morgan held her breath as she followed Willie out into the hallway, then down the corridor to an empty skybox. Willie held the door for Morgan, and then shut it behind them. She watched his back as he walked over to the floor to ceiling windows, which looked down onto the playing field.

"Ever since I was a little boy I've loved two things with all my heart: women and football. And both bring me great joy and have brought me much pain. But I tell you, something, Morgan," Willie faced her. His eyes seemed glassy, almost watery. Morgan walked over and stood next to him. She placed her hand on his large forearm and nodded.

"Morgan, I love one woman and this whole thing has gotten out of hand. In the beginning it was okay, but now, after talking to my son, this isn't right." Willie ran his large hands over his bald head. "Little Willie called me and asked me questions I hadn't even thought of. Questions about why he, his mother and sister don't live with me. Did I love his mother? Was I giving him another sister, when he really wants a baby brother?" Willie sighed. His large shoulders rose and fell with the emotion. "But, Morgan, the thing that got me was when he said he wanted to be just like me, a big ole pimp!"

Morgan wanted to laugh, but didn't. She saw the pained expression on Willie's face. *Out of the mouths of babes.* She had always adored Willie Junior, the child with the eyes so full of wonder and the easy laugh. If the child had been standing near, she would have grabbed him and hugged him, for his words were just what was needed to get Willie to understand the complexity of just what his actions truly meant, both personally and professionally. She glanced upward and silently thanked God for small favors.

Of all the things Willie could have said. She thought maybe he was going to tell her that he actually had impregnated the woman or that she was one of the many groupies who followed professional teams from town to town and he got caught up with one of them. Instead, his conscious had finally caught up with him in the form of his three-year-old son. Finally, she cheered inwardly. Maybe now she could bill him in a much more positive light, versus the birth control poster boy she'd thought of.

"Willie, listen to that child. How do you think he feels seeing your face plastered across television screens questioning whether or not you are some child's father? And how do you explain the real meaning behind pimp?" Morgan faced Willie and looked up into his warm, brown eyes. Willie had been her first client, had been the one who believed in her when she'd first approached him. In all that time, she had never seen tears form in his eyes.

"Boss Lady," he sniffed as he patted her hand that rested on his forearm and called her by the nickname Tina had lovingly given her. "Those are difficult questions that beg for truthful answers."

Morgan nodded, then crossed the room to the large wet bar. She opened the refrigerator and retrieved two bottles of water. She tossed one bottle to Willie and opened the other. She tilted her head back to take a sip. Her eyes came to rest on a bottle of Parrott's Bay Coconut Rum. She thought of Jarrod. She wondered what he was doing, was he getting ready for tonight's theme night. She faced Willie. "I hear ya. Now, are the allegations true?"

"No, Morgan, that woman is lying. She's accusing me because Raheem turned her down, and I tried to comfort her. I've seen the jazz. I've been like Raheem, enjoyed the status the NFL gave and all its glitz and glory. But I swear to you that I was just trying to comfort her."

"Comfort how, Willie?"

"Put my arm around her. Let her lay her head on my shoulder and cry her eyes out. I even allowed her to camp out in my room for the night."

"Bingo!" Morgan shook her head as she looked at Willie. His face was twisted into a pitiful frown. "Where did you sleep?"

"In the adjoining room. We were in Hawaii at the pro bowl. She was there to hang out with Raheem, but he didn't' want to hang with her. He'd met someone else."

"Unbelievable. You mean to tell me that you're getting accused of some crap that you didn't even do, when in fact the chick is mad at Raheem? How'd she get to Hawaii?"

"Raheem. She's his girlfriend."

A knock on the door interrupted them. Willie shouted for whoever was knocking to go away. The knocking persisted as a voice stated that his press conference was to begin in fifteen minutes.

"I wish you had told me this before now. Why now?"

"Junior. I want him to grow up to be a responsible adult, not a cowardly fool. It takes a coward to lie, and I was willing to lie for Raheem, not thinking of how it would ruin my own life."

Morgan shook her head. She grabbed Willie by his hands. "Okay, Willie. We're going to go out there, and you are going to tell the whole truth."

Willie looked at Morgan. He nodded his head and gave her a slight smile. "Gotcha, Boss Lady. Let's go." He took Morgan by the arm and escorted her to the media room. As they entered, Morgan spotted Raheem at the back of the room. She noted the odd look on his face. A moment later, Willie's girlfriend, Laurina, the mother of his two youngest children, stepped into the room and made her way forward.

Two hours later, the wires had reversed their spin and had labeled the new all-star rookie as the cad of the year, while granting Willie a reprieve, especially after he announced his engagement to Laurina by placing a three carat, emerald cut diamond ring on the third finger of her left hand.

Morgan smiled. Right after the press conference had ended, she'd received a call from Nike. They wanted to talk another deal.

Morgan had wanted to cancel her dinner with Keith Bullock. She had thought a lot about what had just happened with Willie, his admission that things weren't always what they seemed. She thought about Jarrod and his waiting tables. There had to be more to him than just that. His eyes shone with a warm intensity, which spoke about who he was: a warm, caring man. She had made up her mind! The minute she returned, she was going to invite him out and tell him what she did for a living.

As she rushed from her hotel room, she wondered what he was doing this night. As she sat across from a potential new client, Jarrod's light eyes flashed in her mind. Morgan forced herself to pay attention and gave Keith her marketing spiel as she highlighted his on-the-field and off-the-field accomplishments. At the end of dinner, Morgan politely turned down his not-so-subtle hints that she should go out with him.

Back in her hotel room, Morgan took a long hot bath, dressed in a pair of silk pajamas and climbed in bed, pulling the sheet and bed covers over her shoulder. Her lids became heavy as the day's activities wore on her. As she nodded off, she thought of Jarrod again, the solid form of his body, the warm but intense gleam in his light brown eyes. Now, if she could attract a man like him, this whole blind date game would be over. She thought of Willie and wondered had he intentionally set up the meeting with Bullock as a means of hooking her up on a personal level versus professional. True, Bullock agreed to look at her marketing plan for him, but something about the whole evening reeked of setup.

"Oh, no, Willie. Not you, too!" Morgan shook her head, yawned, and then rolled over onto her side. She'd talk to Willie later, but right now she needed sleep. As she finally settled into a deep sleep, she dreamed of the chocolate chip with the light eyes.

"Okay, you want to tell me what gives?" David appeared in the doorway to Nick's bedroom.

Nick raised his head, spied the clock on the nightstand, and then snatched the bed covers over his head.

"Nehemiah called me last night and told me about the sister who spanked him into oblivion. He said that Mr. Johnson told him that her name is Morgan. Is it one in the same?"

Nick tossed the covers from his head and glared at his brother. "Damn, David it's six in the morning. Call me later." He pulled the covers back over his head.

"Jarrod," David called out.

Nick slowly pulled the cover from his head and peered at David. Reluctantly, he sat up.

"Dude, you're trippin'." David sat in a chair near the foot of the bed. "Why would you let that sister believe that you're the damn bartender and not the owner?"

"Mr. Johnson talks too much," Nick mumbled. "Stay out of it." Nick climbed out of bed—naked—and headed to the bathroom. He never wore pajamas to bed. He nearly lost it to the floor when David appeared behind him. "Can I go in peace?" He shoved at his brother with his free hand and slammed the door shut. He cursed loudly.

Finished, he washed his hands, grabbed his robe from the hook on the back of the door and returned to his room. He sat on the edge of the bed.

"Here, I brought you some coffee."

"And I guess I should be grateful." He took the offered Styrofoam cup and sipped the hot brew. The steaming liquid, enhanced with Almond syrup, did little for his body. He hadn't left the bar until well after 4 A.M. He needed more sleep.

"I'll leave after you tell me why the games."

He raked his hand across his face. "You know how sisters can be."

"Bull shit!" David stood and shook his head. "According to Mr. Johnson, this one ain't no chicken head. But more importantly, big brother, game begets game. Remember that. If you want a real sister, you've gotta be real. Later, clown."

If the coffee hadn't tasted so good, he'd of poured it on his brother. Nick scooted to the head of the bed and propped several pillows behind his head. He thought about what David had said and grimaced at his words. True, most sisters wanted a straight up brother, not the game playing type. So, why was he indulging?

His owning Nick's shouldn't be important, but he had found that for some women he'd come across at the bar it was difference between getting just a tip and getting a phone number. If his ownership said phone number, he'd prefer the tip. He wanted a woman to want him for him, not for what he owned.

Nick shook his head, yawned and began to nod. As sleep claimed him, he knew he had to come clean, give her a chance. Besides, not all women were like Tanya or Sheila.

He thought that if Morgan showed up tonight, then he'd tell her who he was and let the chips fall where they may. He rolled over and fell into a fitful sleep as he dreamed of Morgan running away from him.

CHAPTER 8

Morgan stepped into her condo. She placed her overnight near the door, took off her coat, placed it on the hall tree, and then lifted her two pets into her arms. She accepted their brand of affection—Patton's head rub against her cheek and Davis's countless licks across the side of her face. She sighed loudly and placed her pets onto the floor. She kicked off her ankle boots and padded to the kitchen. Patton and Davis close on her heels.

She thought of the success of her trip to Nashville, which had been made so by Willie's truthful admission and his decision to marry his son's mother. She was warmed by the maturity in which he handled the entire situation. Morgan knew that the public, as well as the franchise owners, were becoming increasingly weary of the off the field behavior of their million-dollar babies, and many had begun to show their disdain by including "morality clauses" in player's contracts. Morgan was surprised the Titians hadn't done just that during their last contract negotiations with Willie. And though the casualty of Willie's latest escapade had cost him the initial Nike endorsement deal, the company had come back with another deal, this one just as lucrative as the first offer, with a clause to expand to other Nike merchandise outside of turf shoes.

That deal and the fact that she created marketing and PR plans for not only Willie, but several sports figures, represented all that Morgan wanted Paige Public Relations, Inc. to be.

She smiled as Patton and Davis walked around her. She opened her refrigerator, pulled out a bottle of V-8, then looked up at the calendar on the wall next to the refrigerator. Wednesday. Her date with Lawrence was tonight. Funny, she thought, she had been consumed with Willie and the rampant thoughts of Jarrod that she had not been as excited to meet with Lawrence as she had been a week ago.

She tried to remember what theme night it was at Nicks. She rushed to her home office and began to search for the flier.

"Found it," Morgan called out, then sat at her desk. Tonight was Bid Whist night. Now, that would be something. She wondered if Jarrod even know how to play cards. She sat the flier on the desk then looked down at Patton and Davis as they simultaneously mewed and barked.

"I guess the two of you want a snack." Morgan said as she rose from the desk and headed back to the kitchen. She opened the cabinet and pulled out the treats. Placing their respective treats in front of them, she left the kitchen and headed to her bedroom, pulling her overnight bag behind her. After unpacking, she went into her home office and turned on her computer. As she checked her home and work voice mail messages, she scrolled through her email. She tilted her head to the side when she spotted an email from Lawrence, AKA LawMan1.

"Looking forward to meeting you. I'll be wearing a red jacket. Your Lawman."

Morgan laughed at the moniker. Lawrence was a US Marshall, and from the looks of his picture, what little she could make out, he was built like a brick.

She thought about their meeting and knew she should tell someone about it, but since they were meeting at a public place and Morgan had planned on taking public transportation to the restaurant, which was located at the mouth of the Loop, she didn't see a reason.

Once she finished reading her email and returned several business calls, Morgan decided to take a nap. She climbed into her queen-sized bed, pulled the bead spread over her and shut her eyes. An image of Jarrod crept into her thoughts. And in spite of herself, she smiled wickedly as the innocent thoughts quickly gave way to more intimate ones.

Several hours later, she awoke refreshed. She looked at the clock on the nightstand—the numbers glowed 6:30 in the evening–then stretched, rolling her body from the bed into a standing position. Her feet propelled her forward as she went about taking a quick shower, dabbing her favorite cologne at her pulse points and dressed in a pair of black jeans, with a black turtle neck, a funky pair of red high heel boots she snagged from her favorite shoe store, Sensuous Steps, and a red blazer. She hurried because she didn't want to be late. She abhorred lateness and hoped that Lawrence would be on time.

Morgan put on her full-length leather coat, lined in mink, grabbed her purse then headed out the door for the short walk to the bus stop. As the bus rolled down King Drive, her thoughts vacillated between this blind date with Lawrence and images of Jarrod. She shook her head. She had to think of something else, anything that would move the seemingly unending thoughts of Jarrod to the back of her mind. Morgan allowed Lawrence his just due in her mind. Who knows, she thought, he may just give Jarrod a run for his money and make her forget all about Mr. Bartender. She smirked, "Not!"

Morgan stole another look at her watch. *Not again.* Lawrence, AKA LawMan, was fifteen minutes late. She had arrived at the restaurant early and situated herself near the rear with a bird's eye view of the door. She knew that if he wasn't what he represented, then she'd be able to shimmy to her right, escape to the bathroom, remove her red blazer and make a quick getaway.

She sipped her drink and thought about Jarrod. *Wrong!* Her mind screamed. She was here to meet Lawrence, not think about the fine, chocolate chip brother whose eyes sparkled and sang to her. The more she sipped, the further her bladder protested, until she had no choice but to rush off to the women's bathroom. She hoped Lawrence wouldn't arrive while she was gone.

She rolled her eyes upward when she got to the bathroom and saw the five women waiting in line to use one stall. She thought of using the men's room, which never had a line, but thought better. Besides, she didn't need to go that badly.

Finally, after almost twenty minutes of waiting, she entered the stall. Once finished, she rushed to the sink, washed then dried her hands and stepped quickly out of the bathroom. In her haste, Morgan blindly bumped into the pillow-like feel of a large man.

"Excuse me," she said and stepped around him.

"Morgan?" She heard her name and turned slowly. The first thing she saw were the light beige hands. She didn't want to look up, didn't want to know. "Morgan? Spin Master?" He called her by her screen name. Tentatively, she raised her eyes. Instantly, she wanted to scream.

"It's me. It's your LawMan."

If ever there was a moment when Morgan wanted to just run like hell's fire was at her feet, this was as good a time as any, but decorum kept her rooted. She plastered a smile on her face and looked up into the steel blue eyes smiling down at her. Her eyes trailed upward and rested on the sparse grey hair, wisps pulled over to one side in a sad attempt to hide his bald spot. Now, she wanted to cry.

"Umm, ahh..." She was at a loss of words as she continued to look at the man who, for sure, was nothing like the picture, grainy as all get out, she had looked at. His large cheeks were a rosy red, and his narrow nose jutted out the same distance as his chin.

Morgan wasn't prejudiced, not in the least, but she had never given much thought to dating outside of her race—to her, dating men who looked much like her father was a given.

"Sorry I'm late. Traffic was maddening," he said and smiled, then covered his mouth. Morgan tried not to stare, but she could have sworn that his teeth moved. "Have you eaten yet?"

Morgan shook her head. She was still too taken aback to speak. Never in her wildest dreams, imagined or real, would she have thought that Lawrence was white! She may have been able to forgive him had he looked more like Matthew McConaughey than a puffed up version of Boris Badenov. Where was Yavette when she needed her? She began to will her cell phone to ring, vibrate, something that would give her an excuse to leave.

"I know you're surprised, but I'm on a diet. I'm gonna lose these last pounds."

One hundred may do, she wanted to say.

"You look just like your picture. Come on." He grabbed her hand, and she wanted to squirm. His hand was wet and clammy. Hadn't he just left the bathroom?

Quietly, Morgan allowed her dream date to escort her to a table. He held the seat for her before he sat down across from her. "So, tell me how your day was?"

Great, until I came here.

She wanted to be mean, but she just couldn't bring herself to do so. It wasn't his fault. It was all hers. She knew when she got the picture that she should have insisted on a recent, clearer photo of him.

Morgan's eyes were drawn to his mouth once more. *There! His teeth did move.*

"My day was fine. And yours?" She had to see it one more time to make sure her mind wasn't playing tricks on her.

She watched his thin upper lip stretch across his teeth. The teeth didn't move. When the server appeared she placed two glasses of white wine on their table then took their order, Lawrence ordered for both of them. Morgan frowned. He hadn't even looked her way—hadn't asked her what she wanted to eat.

Morgan's mind spun. How was she going to get out of here without being rude?

Maybe a headache? No, too obvious. How about a sick parent? No, don't want to lie on mom and dad—they're healthier than a pair of oxen.

How about the truth? Just tell him the truth. That I don't date outside of my race. Skip the fact that he's bald, pudgy and just plain not my type.

The server arrived and sat a plate in front of Morgan just as she was about to tell Lawrence the truth.

"Eat up. We don't want that great figure to go to waste." He smiled, his jaws wiggled.

There! His teeth did move.

Morgan spied at him between picks at her plate of mixed green salad with vinegar dressing. She was stunned when the server returned moments later and placed in front of Lawrence a large porterhouse steak, topped with braised mushrooms, accompanied by several garlic bread sticks, a small bowl of broccoli and a large baked potato, teaming with butter and sour cream.

What did I do wrong to deserve this? I never kicked my cat. I was never mean to anyone. Obeyed my parents and never lied on my taxes. So why am I being punished with the blind dates from hell? I gotta get out of here. Morgan looked around the restaurant. She looked at her watch. It wasn't too late to head to Nick's. If she remembered correctly, the Bid Whist games wouldn't start until after eight. If she left now, she'd be able to sign up to play a few hands. *Oh right,* she thought, *who am I kidding?* She was headed to Nick's to see Jarrod, tell him who she was, and then ask him out on a date.

Morgan looked up at Lawrence when she heard the sound of something plopping. She watched in amusement as he covered his mouth with his left hand as his right fished around in the wine glass for his teeth. Morgan tried not to laugh, for the look on Lawrence's face tugged at her heart, but with his fingers trying to grasp the false teeth, she couldn't help the giggle that burst forth.

"Here, Lawrence." Morgan picked up a spoon, tilted the glass and maneuvered the teeth from the glass onto a napkin. She slid the napkin toward him.

After he adjusted his teeth, he smiled brightly at her. Morgan shook her head.

"Lawrence," she began, "I have to go."

"What's wrong?" he asked. She noticed that the lines in his forehead became more pronounced. "I thought we were just gelling."

"I have to be honest with you."

He interrupted her. "It's the hair and teeth isn't it? I just forgot the bond. And I'm having a hair transplant next week."

Morgan patted his hand. "No, Lawrence, that's not it. I've got southern parents and was raised with southern ways." She looked into his eyes. She had to admit they were a beautiful blue, but that didn't make up for what she knew she would never feel for him, or the rest of him for that matter.

"Okay, so? My parents are from Alabama."

"Are they still alive?"

"No, God rest their souls. Lost them both five years ago, one month after the other."

"Sorry to hear that, Lawrence. But if they were alive, would you be able to take me to their house for dinner?"

Lawrence looked away. "They wouldn't understand."

"Well, mine are still alive and neither would they." He looked at her. "As a matter of fact, Lawrence, I've never dated outside of my race, and I've never really been interested in doing so. But thank you for dinner and take care. Good luck."

She stood, opened her red Coach, placed several bills on the table and headed toward the exit. Morgan turned at the sound of her name.

"Morgan, I understand. Thank you just the same for meeting me. I haven't been out with a beautiful woman in a long time. Maybe we can be friends?" He placed the bills in her hand.

She looked up at him. She wanted to say "sure;" but she knew that it would be a lie. Still, she could just this one time. No. She didn't want to give him false hope nor make any insinuations that they would continue to chat past this night. "Lawrence, I'd be lying if I said yes."

He nodded his head. "I see. Well, good night Morgan. Spin Master."

"Night, Lawman."

Morgan hailed a cab.

"Nick's Sport's Bar and Grille on 71st Street." She waved to Lawrence as the cab sped from the curb.

CHAPTER 9

Morgan waltzed into Nick's. Craig wasn't at the door when she arrived. Another bouncer greeted her. Though not as warm as Craig, his thick neck and arms were as much a deterrent to crime as Craig's. Morgan smiled at him as he held the door for her and mumbled "Welcome to Nick's. I'm Devon."

She nodded her head, stepped inside the club, and then looked around, her eyes searching for Jarrod.

"Well, if it isn't the woman who killed my pride and spanked me good on the dance floor." Nehemiah stood next to Morgan.

"Wow. I didn't know you were so sensitive. Had I known, I would have only spanked you a little bit and not a lot."

Nehemiah raised his eyebrows, then threw his head back in laughter. "I guess you told me. How are you tonight?"

"Well. And you?"

"No complaints. Looks like we're going to pack them in tonight."

Morgan looked around. Yes, she thought, that they were. But she was interested in one thing—Jarrod.

"Oh, he's off tonight." Nehemiah seemed to have read her thoughts, but she couldn't go out like that. She looked up into his eyes. "Who's off tonight?" She placed her manicured hand on her chest. Her heart sank and she hoped that he hadn't seen the disappointment in her eyes. She heard him chuckled slightly before answering and she knew he wasn't going to let her off that easy.

"My brother, Ni… I mean, Jarrod," he replied. She watched him as he peered at her and thought that it was no big deal to mix up a name, everyone mixes up names sometimes, and she wondered why he blanched.

"Hey, I can make a mean drink. Why don't you sit in your favorite area, and I'll fix you a drink. Coconut rum with pineapple juice. Correct?"

Morgan nodded her head, and then walked slowly to the Sports Arena. She sat at the table she'd last shared with Tina and Mr. Johnson. She glanced around the room as her head absently bobbed to the smooth music that seeped from the large speakers. She wanted to leave—the object of her waking thoughts was nowhere to be found.

Nehemiah rushed into the office, picked up the phone and quickly dialed his brother's phone number. When he got no answer at the home number, he called Nick's cell phone number. Getting no answer there either, he called the home number again and left a message for Nick to call him ASAP. Nehemiah came from the office, retrieved Morgan's drink and headed toward her table. He shook his head. If his brother got a look at this sister tonight, he'd not only tell her who he was, but would quickly make sure that no one else would step to her. As he neared, he spied some dude sitting at the table with her.

Oh, no, this one is Nick's, Nehemiah thought. His eyes narrowed as he neared and heard the man tell Morgan that her man was a fool to let her out by herself.

"Oh, dude! My bad," Nehemiah said as he let the contents of Morgan's drink slosh onto the lap of her table mate. He jumped up as the cool liquid quickly made a large dark wet spot near his groin and down the left leg of his tan corduroys.

"Hey, the bathroom is in the back to your left," Nehemiah said as he looked up into his face. Nehemiah detected the dude wanted to say something, but at 6'4", and a solid two hundred-fifty pounds, few men said anything out of the way to Nehemiah. Instead, he rushed away toward the bathroom.

"I can be awfully clumsy," Nehemiah winked at Morgan. "I'll get you another drink. Be right back." He rushed off, barked out the order for another drink to the barmaid, and went into the office. He called Nick again. He cursed under his breath when he got his brother's voice mail again. He walked out of the office, grabbed the drink and headed back to where Morgan was sitting. As he neared, he saw the form of another man sitting with her, his back to Nehemiah as he sat a little too close. This was getting expensive, Nehemiah muttered but knew that his brother really liked this one and just needed a little interference to push them a long. So, what if he'd have to dump twenty drinks in the laps of any man who dared sit with Morgan.

As Nehemiah got to the table and just before he tipped the glass, he looked down.

"What's up?" Nick said to Nehemiah. "How're things going tonight?"

"It's all good. What's up with you?" Nehemiah looked at his brother, then looked to Morgan. She sat there, a smile plastered on her face. Yeah, Nehemiah thought, that's how he liked seeing her—the disappointed look earlier tugged at his heart. He didn't want to ever see sadness in her eyes.

"Oh, nothing. Thought I'd come in here and brush up on my card playing skills."

"Y'all want something to drink? I'll be right back."

They both looked at Nehemiah's retreating back, then chuckled.

Nick looked at Morgan. He loved the way her twists kissed the nape of her neck, her smooth complexion, and those deep, brown eyes. He wanted to reach out and stroke the side of her face with his thumb. "How are you tonight, Morgan?"

"I'm okay. You?"

He scooted his chair closer. "I'll be better once I hear if you've got a date Friday night?"

Morgan didn't want to believe her ears. Had she just heard him right? she wondered. Had he truly asked her if she had a date?

"Umm, no. I don't. Why?"

He looked into her eyes. Yes, this was how he wanted them to start. "Cause if you don't, I'd—"

Nehemiah appeared and interrupted Nick. "Umm, can I talk to you for a minute? Morgan, do you mind?"

She looked from Nehemiah to Jarrod. "No, not at all."

"Thanks. And put this glass in that seat." He handed her the drink and winked at her as he tapped his brother on the shoulder and pointed toward the men's room. As they neared, the man Nehemiah poured the drink on stepped out of the bathroom. The stain had crept up toward his waist. "My bad. You cool? Send us the cleaning bill."

Nick looked from the man to Nehemiah and raised his eyebrows.

"I'll explain later. Come on," Nehemiah said as they continued until they were in the storage room at the very back of the bar. Nehemiah opened the door leading into the alley. Nick shook his head. Both of his brothers were given to dramatics!

"Man, I've called every phone you have. Where've you been?"

Nick looked down at the cell phone attached to his hip. He noticed it was off.

"My fault. I thought I turned the phone on. I'm here now. What's the matter?"

"I wanted you to know that Morgan had come by." Nehemiah nodded his head to one side and raised his right eyebrow. Nick looked at the strange expression on his brother's face.

"Okay. So?"

"Boy you thick! She likes you. She didn't come in here looking for me. She came looking for you." He tapped Nick on the shoulder. "So its time to step up to the plate, my brother. But if you're going to go out there and continue this masquerade as Jarrod, then I'm going to go out there and tell her myself."

"Nehemiah, I'm gonna come clean. I'm going to ask her out. Tell her my whole name."

"I'd sure do hope so, 'cause she's really nice. And her girl, Tina, speaks highly of her. As a matter of fact, Tina works for Morgan. She—"

Just as he started to tell Nick all about Morgan's cousin and Jackson, and how he was going to be her date, their attention was grasped by the sound of a loud commotion. They rushed through the doors. As they entered the main area, both were astonished to see two women fighting. Nick headed toward the two women just as Devon reached them and separated them. Nick escorted one woman to the back office, while Devon escorted the other to the rear store room.

After a half hour of processing, where by the women's ID were copied and their pictures were taken, they were each given a gentle, but persuasive, suggestion that neither return to Nick's Sports Bar & Grille. Nick exited the office and began to search for Morgan. He was taking his brother's advice and was going to tell her that he was the owner, not just the bartender-slash-waiter. He looked around the bar but didn't see her. He even went outside in hopes of maybe catching a glimpse of her Jaguar. He frowned when he didn't see her car and walked back into the bar.

"Is she gone?" Nehemiah came to stand next to Nick, who simply nodded his head before speaking.

"Seems that way." He looked around the bar one last time. "You mind if I don't stay around to help close up tonight? I think I'm going to head home."

Nehemiah looked at his younger brother. He knew the pain of wanting something so bad that all you could do was think of it day and night. He thought of the one woman who had once claimed his heart, right before his accident. He knew when he married that he'd done so on the rebound. Sierra had asked him if they have a future, but he had been so hell-bent on proving what a player he was that he'd lost the one woman who'd made him truly love. Nehemiah smiled ruefully, then thought about Tina. Something about Tina reminded him of Sierra. Though they looked nothing alike, they both seemed to possess a deep abiding self-love that he found exhilarating and fearful at the same time. No, he wouldn't allow Nick to loose out on a good thing. He'd give him another week, and then he'd have to just fix them up with Tina's assistance.

"No I don't mind. Go on home. I'll talk to you later." Nehemiah patted Nick on the back and watched as he exited the bar, his shoulders slightly slumped.

Nick climbed onto his motorcycle and headed home. He'd had no idea Morgan would be at the bar. So when he walked in and saw her sitting alone, looking damn good as always, he knew it was no coincidence. But he couldn't believe that his bad luck would turn to worse. First the brother with the drink on his pants, of which he found out later, Nehemiah purposely tipped into his lap to get him to vacate the seat next to Morgan, followed by the two women fighting, ending with Morgan disappearing. This was too much, he thought as he sped toward home. Skip waiting until Jackson's little party. He didn't want to waste another moment. Besides, he wanted to end those blind dates she was supposed to go on courtesy of her cousin Yavette. He wanted to be her one and only date—the man she was looking for, knew that he could love her like no other. Yeah, it was time. Plus he didn't want her to think that he was a liar yet, that was exactly what he was being when he'd neglected to tell her who he was.

He pulled into the driveway and parked his bike within the wrought iron gate. Slowly, he climbed the steps to his home. Once inside, he tossed his keys onto the foyer table and headed up the stairs to his bedroom. As he undressed, he rehearsed how he'd tell her then where he'd take her for their first date. His last thought as he laid his head on the pillow was her beautiful, smooth chestnut complexion and the sweet smile she gave him each time he'd seen her.

"I've got one more day to make this right," he said as he lay on his back and stared at the ceiling. He knew that first thing in the morning, he'd get up and call Jackson. He needed ammunition—needed to know a few more things about Morgan in order to get ready for their date. Oh, he was going to woo her well before the card party; just wanted to make sure that when she saw he was her final date it would be hard for her to even think about turning him down.

For hours thereafter, Nick lay in bed and stared into dark nothingness, his mind racing in and out of the one woman he wanted to get to know, wanted to see her sensuous smile, smell that wicked perfume, and hear her warm voice speak his name. Nick chuckled, thinking that he had a serious case of womanitis! Bad! He rolled over on his side and yawned as he felt his eyelids become heavy. As sleep began to claim him, his last thought was of him holding Morgan close to his heart.

Morgan hadn't wanted to wait until the theatrics between the two women died down. After her unwanted seatmate returned from the bathroom, she watched in utter amazement as the two women marched into the bar and stepped right up to her former seatmate. Her head went from one woman to the next as they jockeyed for his attention. Things heated up when the caramel hued woman grabbed Mr. Seatmate. That's when the other woman, dressed in a red, form-fitting velveteen dress, grabbed Ms. Caramel's hand. It was on! Ms. Caramel reared back and slapped Ms. Velveteen, who in turn slugged Ms. Caramel. In a matter of seconds, both were on the floor tussling like wrestlers. Morgan tried not to laugh, for she really did find it distasteful to fight over men, but no one stifled so much as a grin when Ms. Caramel's wig came off, followed by Ms. Velveteen's phony pony, tossed across the room.

She had made her way to the exit just as she spotted Jarrod and Nehemiah heading toward the fight. Once last glance was all it took as Morgan stepped outside, looked up and down the street, and upon seeing a cab, hailed the vehicle, jumped in and headed home.

The light night traffic was a welcome and the cabbie didn't seem to be in a hurry as they usually are. She thought of Jarrod, the intensity in his warm, light eyes and he sat next to her, pulling his chair closer, then put his hand on top of hers. She could see he had something to say and her heart had beat a million times a minute, sweat beads formed across her upper lips. She'd wanted him to hurry, for she had something she wanted to say, needed to say.

How ironic, she thought, she'd just been thinking of him, wondered where he was as the soft music seeped out of the speakers nice and slow. She pictured herself in his arms, swaying slowly side to side, her head resting on his large chest. And her day dream had been unhappily interrupted first by her unwanted tablemate followed by Nehemiah pouring her drink into her tablemate's lap. She hadn't a clue that he was up to something until she spied Nehemiah wink at her as her tablemate rushed to the bathroom.

Then, just as Jarrod moved his body closer to hers, his cologne a mixture of patchouli and his natural body scent, his eyes slightly shielded by his long eyelashes, here come Nehemiah, then all hell broke loose with the fight.

After paying the cabbie, Morgan headed up to her condo, hearing the mewls and whimpers of her two pets as she stepped off the elevator. Once inside, she picked them both up and carried them into her room. Placing them on the bed, she put on her nightgown and slid between the sheets. A slight shiver stole its way across her as she thought of Jarrod—the way his shirt fit his chest and arms, the warm, yet intense light eyes and the nefarious, boyish smile, dimples and all. *Yeah*, she thought, *a brother like Jarrod is just my speed.* He seemed nice, quite charming and a little protective—just like she liked them. No, he didn't seem to be a push over—couldn't be, not working with the public. But there seemed to be more to him. Something different. Something that set him apart. Morgan just didn't know what it was.

Morgan floated in her thoughts until the realization that the next day, Thursday, she had a date with Tony. Again, an odd dread she hadn't experienced before crept up her spine. She had agreed to meet him and would go through with the date. She wondered if Yavette's words would come true, that Tony would be her last date. She wasn't too sure how she felt about that. If he turned out to be a bust, then she'd say no to a third blind date and ask Jarrod out. But if he turned out to be a real nice person, who was warm and sensitive and built like Jarrod, then she was in trouble.

Morgan stretched her arms as Patton jumped onto the bed and assumed her spot, followed by Gen. Davis, who did likewise. Eyes heavy with sleep, Morgan rolled over and shut her eyes, allowing sleep to claim her. As she finally drifted off, she thought of the handsome chocolate chip—not her upcoming blind date with Tony.

CHAPTER 10

Morgan woke early and headed into the office. As she arrived, she noted that Tina was already there.

"What brings you in so early?" Morgan asked as she stopped at Tina's desk. She noticed the large vase of flowers sitting on its corner. "Those are beautiful. Who sent them?"

Tina smiled as she leaned over and inhaled the fragrance from the mixture of roses and baby's breath. "Nehemiah." She responded.

Morgan laughed as she watched the dreamy state her assistant's eyes took on. She hadn't felt that way in a long time. "Wow. So, am I to assume that you and Nehemiah exchanged numbers?"

"Yes, and we're going out tonight to a little spot up north."

Morgan couldn't contain her large grin. She was grinning for both Tina and Nehemiah. She hadn't gotten any strange vibes from Nehemiah, and though his personality was a little more outgoing than Jarrod's, she found him quite charming and engaging.

"Now, that sounds great." She looked at Tina's hands. Her nails, though neat and clean, Morgan felt could stand a good manicure. She looked at Tina's stylish Afro. A nice trim would be wonderful. "Hey, you've been great, holding down the fort while I'm gone and helping me keep afloat. I want to treat you today."

"Aww, Boss Lady, no need. We've way too much work around here today."

Morgan raised an eyebrow. She knew that Tina was attempting to change her mind. No way! Her mind was made up. She was going to treat Tina to a day at the spa and hair stylist. She rounded Tina's desk, flipped through the rolodex and found her girlfriend's number.

Picking up the phone on the desk, she punched in the number and tapped her boot-clad foot on the carpet. "Good morning, this is Morgan

Paige. Is Bambi available?" She put her hand up, and then turned her back on Tina when Tina began to protest. "Hey, Bambi. Girl, I'm sending my executive assistant over there for the works. She's got a hot date tonight, and I want you to hook my girl up! And add it my account. What time should I send her?" Morgan tapped her fingertips on the deep, mahogany desk. "In an hour. Girl, she's on her way! Thank you, Bambi, girl, you're a doll. And I'll see you in a couple of weeks." Morgan hung up the phone then turned to Tina.

"Get out of that seat, put on your coat and head on over to Honey Chile's. My girl is waiting for you." Morgan pulled Tina's seat out and gently took her under her arm. "And I'll see you Monday. Take tomorrow off."

"But…" Tina tried to protest as Morgan placed her coat about her shoulders.

Morgan laughed at the shocked expression on Tina's face.

"Get out," Morgan ordered and pointed toward the door. "And don't you dare call me at all today. Call me tomorrow to tell me about your date."

Morgan pushed Tina out of the door, then stepped into her office. She looked out of the window and smiled. The cool autumn weather was just her speed. The crispness in the air, the way the leaves turned beautiful shades of orange, gold, and brown. She tore herself from the window and sat down at her desk. Tina had already checked her voice mail, and had placed the messages on her desk. She looked through them and saw a message from Tony among the stack. "Dang, the date's tonight."

She placed the note to the side. She resolved to call him later as a mental image of Jarrod popped into her head. She knew the next time she was in his company she'd ask him out. And if she didn't know any better, that was going to be Friday. She'd make it tonight, Thursday, but she had made the date with Tony.

Morgan forced all thoughts of the blind date with Tony and the sensuous image of Jarrod from her mind, and began working in earnest on a marketing plan for her new client.

Nick stood outside of his friend's floral shop. He wanted the arrangement to be special, seeing as how Jackson's fiancée, Yavette, was at Jackson's this morning when he called at five. He knew that Jackson would think he had lost his mind, but he knew he wanted to take this first step. As he spoke with Yavette, he'd gotten a little angry when she informed him that Morgan had a blind date tonight! Once he hung up, he knew that even though Yavette promised he'd be Morgan's third blind date, he knew he couldn't leave it to chance—he had to pre-empt the strike, and what better way than with a bouquet of flowers to let her know that he was thinking of her. He knew it was risky—for if he signed the card, she'd really wonder how he got all of information. But if he didn't sign it, she may think it was from one of her blind dates, and he sure as hell didn't want to give either one of those losers credit— losers because they were going to lose Morgan.

After placing the order, he headed back home to get some rest. Tonight was Steppers Night, and according to Nehemiah, folks loved to step and would crowd the place out. And though he wouldn't be there all night, he wanted to at least close up. Nehemiah said he had a date and wouldn't be able to close. David had agreed to bartend tonight, but needed to be out before the last call for alcohol at 2 A.M. On one hand he'd hoped Morgan would stop by, yet on the other, if she did and he wasn't there, he wouldn't get a chance to ask her to her face, again, if she was free on Friday night. Well, either way, he knew where to call her on Friday morning to ensure they had a date.

Morgan stretched her arms above her head. She had been sitting at her computer for four hours without a break. As she rounded her desk, she looked up to see one of her employees enter her office with a large floral arrangement.

"Thanks, Sean. Put those on Tina's desk."

"Why? They've got your name on it."

Morgan raised her eyebrows and then pointed to herself. "Me?"

Sean nodded, then smiled. "I wish my partner would send me flowers. Y'all wouldn't care, would you?"

"No," she responded absently as she stepped forward to accept the wrapped package. She pulled the white paper from the package and gasped when she pulled a large white bear from atop a wicker basket. She smiled brightly as she looked at the basket brimming with blooming African violet, azalea, miniature red and white roses, hypostases plants and a small green ivy plant. She searched frantically for the card.

"This is just the beginning—N. J. Chambers, Jr." Morgan read the card and tried to think of anyone she knew with the last name Chambers: a client, a friend from college, a casual acquaintance. She couldn't think of a soul with the last name Chambers. She turned the card over and saw the florist's name on it—Edmunds House of Flowers. She called the number listed, spoke with the owner and was politely, yet firmly, told that they do not give out personal information unless she felt threatened. And Morgan felt far from threatened. Curious? Yes. Impressed? For sure. But not threatened. She hung up and looked up to see Sean still standing in her office.

"Ms. Paige has a secret admirer. Now that's sweet."

"I guess. Cause I sure don't have a clue."

At the sound of the phone ringing, Morgan sat the basket on her desk and picked up the phone.

"Paige PR," she responded into the handset.

"Wow, what a beautiful voice." She heard a man say. "And I know you are as beautiful as you sound. How you doin'?" The male voice asked.

"Good. Who is this?"

"Your date!"

Morgan breathed out slowly as she sat down behind her desk. "Hi, Tony, how are you?"

"I'll be better once I see you tonight. Are we still on?"

"Sure we are. Where, and what time, do you want to meet?"

"How about this little hole in the wall I know. Nick's Sports Bar and Grille, around seven o'clock. Then we can go to dinner from there."

Morgan broke out into a cold sweat. There was no way she was going to meet Tony at Nick's. No way! She had to think up something fast. But what? Umm, her mind raced as she tried to think up a believable reason why they couldn't meet at Nick's outside of the truth—she didn't want Jarrod to see her with a date, blind or otherwise.

"What did you have in mind for dinner?" she asked.

"How about we see what you want to eat?"

Dang! He wasn't making this easy. "Well, I like Chinese, Ethiopian, Italian, American fare. I'm not picky. But we don't have to meet at Nick's."

She heard Tony take a sharp breath in. "I'm scheduled to have a meeting there, and my car is in the shop, so if you don't mind, I'd like to meet there."

Morgan's mouth formed a pout. How in the world would she get out of this? She could play suddenly stricken with bubonic plague. No, that was arrested over 100 years ago with the invention of penicillin. *Okay, think,* Morgan chided herself. She heard him call her name.

"I've got to go. I'll see you at Nick's at seven. Do you know where the joint is?"

Morgan nodded. "Umm, yeah. See ya."

"Can't wait, sweetheart. I'll be dressed in a grey, pin-striped suit, with a black cashmere overcoat, cowboy boots and hat. See you at seven. Ciao."

"Bye." She hung up the phone, and then slumped down into her chair and hid her face in her hands. She heard Sean clear his throat. She looked up to see him sitting across from her. Sean had worked with her for the past four years as an account representative. She hired him after she picked up her fifth professional sports client. Sean was responsible for finding new opportunities, and talking companies into allowing her clients to promote their products.

"I'm sunk," Morgan breathed out, then shook her head. Of all the nightclubs and bars in Chicago, this man had to pick Nick's! Where Jarrod, the brother who had slid into her dreams and got under her skin, worked just about every day. Had she taken the bull by the horns last night, she would have known not only where he lives, his phone number, but what days he works at Nick's.

"It can't be that bad," Sean responded. Morgan shook her head. She didn't want to get into it—didn't want her employees, not even Tina, whom she trusted, to know she had resorted to blind dates, while also falling for a bartender with a sensuous aura, wicked dimpled smile and a body to rival LL Cool J's. She looked up at Sean and rose from her chair.

"No, Sean, it's not. I can handle it. But I don't really want to talk about it right now. Thanks for bringing in the flowers."

"Not a problem. I also have the specs for Mr. Bullock. Would you like to go over them?"

Morgan nodded her head and watched as Sean rushed from the office and returned moments later with a red folder—his color for hot prospect. For over an hour the two discussed the various products their newest client could endorse. At the end, they had decided to pursue two cellular phone companies and a charity for children, to begin with.

The ringing of Morgan's private line caught her attention. She looked down at the caller-ID unit and saw her parent's home phone number appear on the unit. She picked up the receiver.

"Hi, I was thinking about you guys earlier. How's things?"

"Good, Sweetie. We didn't hear from you when you got back from Nashville. How'd it go?" Ishmael Paige asked his only child.

"It went really well, Dad. And I picked up another client. Keith Bullock."

"That's great, Morgan. Does he drink like Willie?"

Morgan rolled her eyes heavenward. There was just no way around this conversation. Her father was incorrigible when it came to liquor. To Morgan, her father was not only a good man, but a great dad and minister as well. Growing up, she didn't feel the pressure most children of ministers endured. Reverend Ishmael Paige wanted her to grow up with a healthy love and respect for her faith, not "a blinding commitment," to the church. Yet, to Morgan, her father had one flaw—he was obsessed with the effects of liquor. She understood it had a lot to do with Grandpa Mack, her father's father, but she also felt that he should move forward and truly forgive. Every opportunity he got, he preached about how liquor leads one to sin, especially when you imbibe too much.

"Dad, Willie drinks about as much as I do," she responded, then shut her eyes tightly. Though her father knew her business took her to establishments that served liquor, he thought she didn't touch the stuff. *Well, the cat's out of the bag now. Might as well get on with it.* "Besides, it's not a sin to drink. It's a sin to become drunk."

"Child, do not tell me what a sin is and what isn't. I watched what liquor can do to a person."

Morgan sighed heavily. This was one conversation she always tried to avoid. "Okay, Daddy. I'm not going to argue with you today."

"And I'm not going to argue with you either. Just tell me you don't hang out at bars like a harlot, sitting around with a drink in your hand."

Morgan sure wanted to lie. *He must have a crystal ball,* she thought. *How does he know I sit at a bar with a drink in my hand?* "I'm not going to lie to you. I do. I like to go out, and yes, I have one drink. But I'm no harlot, and I don't stumble out the joint with a brotha on my arm for a one night stand. I go back the next day and get him." She snickered, knowing her father wouldn't appreciate her wayward humor. She sobered when he didn't respond. "Dad? You still there?"

"Let me let you speak with your mother. Goodbye."

"Hi, Morgan. What did you do to get the good reverend on the liquor rant?"

"Told him the truth, that I go to a bar and have a drink."

Morgan heard her mother sigh out loud. Norma Paige was typically quiet, that was until you got her husband riled up. "Why did you have to go and do that? Now I've got to listen to this sermon for hours on end. And you know I'm not trying to hear it."

"Sorry, Mom, but he asked, and I wasn't going to lie."

Morgan went on to tell her mother about Willie and her new clients. Norma ended their conversation by asking Morgan if she knew that Yavette was getting married.

"So why didn't you call and tell me? Etta called yesterday and told us," Norma whispered into the phone.

"Mom, why are you whispering?"

"Your father is still on the liquor rant. If he knew I wasn't paying attention, then he'd start over. And if he does, I'm moving in with you and your animals will have to vacate."

Morgan snickered. "They haven't set a date or anything. I think she said something about having a little get-together before the official engagement party."

"Baby," Norma began. Morgan steeled herself. She wasn't sure what her mother was about to say, but the syrupy sound was a usual signal that she wanted Morgan to do her a favor.

"Yes, Mother," she replied cautiously.

"What about you, dear? Got any prospects? Anyone worthy of marriage?"

Morgan's mouth dropped open wide. Her mother was the last person she'd expect to ask about her dating life. Usually it was her father who asked all the dating questions. She didn't even know how to respond.

"Ummm, jeez, Mom, no. There is no one special. No prospects." She looked at the basket and thought that, whoever Mr. Chambers was, he had damn good taste. *Maybe this was the prospect.* She averted her eyes to the clock sitting on the wall. It was past two, and she needed to head home and get ready for her second blind date. "Mom, I've gotta run. I need to wrap it up around here. I'll talk to you later, and kiss Daddy for me."

"Okay. Take care and God's blessings."

"Same to you." Morgan placed the receiver on its base. She no longer felt like working, knowing she had put in nearly eight hours already. She wasn't going to do ten, not today. She called out to Sean. When he appeared in the doorway, she said, "I'm out of here for the rest of the day. If any thing crazy jumps off, hit me on my cell phone."

"Gotcha, Boss Lady. Have a great evening."

Morgan looked at Sean. Did he know about her blind dates? Her eyes narrowed. *Crazy,* she chided herself, *just plain old crazy. He doesn't know a thing.*

"Thanks Sean. I'll see you in the morning."

"Yes, Boss Lady."

Morgan stepped outside, pulled her collar up around her neck and headed to the parking garage. As she waited for the vehicles ahead of her to move toward the exit, she thought of Tony and Jarrod. One she knew and the other she hadn't a clue about. Jarrod's eyes spoke of passion, while this Tony, so far, had only been words. Jarrod's smile put her at east, while Tony, well, she hadn't met him so she really couldn't say. She dismissed the game as she exited the garage and headed home to get ready for her date with Tony.

CHAPTER 11

"Good evening, Morgan. Glad to see you again." Craig held open the door of the cab, and then escorted her into the bar.

Morgan smiled and nodded her head at Craig as she stood near the entrance and let her eyes scan the crowd. She knew who she was looking for, and she hadn't seen him. The rapid beating of her heart slowed a little. She knew Nehemiah wouldn't be at the bar. He was out with Tina.

"Miss Morgan," Mr. Johnson came to stand in front of her. She smiled and hugged him. She needed to sooth her nerves. "What's wrong?" He looked into her eyes.

"Oh, nothing. I'm, umm, waiting."

"Waiting for what. Or should I say who?"

"I umm, got a date."

"Hot dang—told that boy not to wait. Where y'all going?"

Morgan tilted her head to one side. "Mr. Johnson, who are you talking about?"

"Nicky!"

"Nicky, who?"

She watched as odd emotions appeared on Mr. Johnson's face. "Wait, didn't you tell me your date's name?" Mr. Johnson stammered.

"No, sir. You okay?" She looked at him as his eyes seemed to narrow. "Come on over here and sit down." Morgan looped her arm through Mr. Johnson's. "Let's get you something to drink." Morgan raised her hand and nearly choked when a Jarrod look-a-like stopped at their table.

"Hey, Mr. Johnson. What can I get you and the lovely lady?"

Mr. Johnson looked up. "Hello, David. Get me a ginger ale with cherries, heavy on the cherries. And my friend, Morgan, will take a Parrot Bay rum with pineapple juice, heavy on the juice."

"No, skip the rum. Bring me a ..." her voice trailed off as she looked up. She knew she was staring, but she couldn't help it. The man looked just like Jarrod. She watched as he extended his hand to her.

"It's a pleasure to finally meet the woman that one of my bothers is smitten with and the other got his behind spanked on the dance floor. My name is David. I'm the youngest between the three."

"Nice to meet you. You and Jarrod could almost be twins."

"Lots of people tell us that. What would you like to drink?"

"Oh, that's right, I didn't finish. I'll take the same thing Mr. Johnson's having, including the cherries."

"Gotcha. I'll be right back with your drink."

Dang, what is this, a family affair? Morgan thought then looked at Mr. Johnson.

"Okay, Miss Morgan, I've got my senses. Had my folks mixed up. You said you got a date. With who?"

How was she going to tell Mr. Johnson that, though she and Tony had spoken a couple of times on the telephone, they had never met. Outside of Yavette, and now Jackson, no one knew she had been going on blind dates. Maybe it was time to toss this madness onto someone else and get their take on the whole thing.

"Let me ask you, Mr. Johnson, are you married?"

"Yes, I am. And have been for over thirty years. Jean is the love of my life."

Morgan smiled. "How did you two meet?"

"On a blind date."

She scrunched up her face. "Are you for real?"

"Yup, met right here. She was friends with Nick Senior. He introduced us, and we were like glue from that day forward. I don't know what I'd do without her. She's not much into bar scenes, but she does come in here every once in a while. Why you ask?"

"I ...." She began. "I'm here to meet another blind date," she spat out then frowned.

"Another?"

They became quiet as David appeared with their drinks. He smiled, a lot like Jarrod's as he walked away. Morgan looked at him, then her watch. It was seven-fifteen. Tony was late. She looked up into Mr. Johnson's deep brown eyes. "Yeah, another." She replied and saw understanding in the eyes staring back at her. She had a sudden urge to unleash, a need to tell the incredible stories in hopes that someone else other than herself would tell her that she was crazy. "Well, the first date and this one was set up by my cousin, Yavette. And I had one from the Internet. I've got one more. Yet, for the life of me, I don't know why I let her talk me into these blind dates. I have enough on my plate as it is."

Morgan went on to tell Mr. Johnson about her company, Paige's Public & Media Relations, before she continued to tell him all about her last two blind dates.

"So you see, Mr. Johnson, I'm not sure I can stand another one. And this one is late."

"Why don't you tell your cousin you've changed mind. And when this guy shows up, tell him you've got a date with me?" he asked, his eyes wide as his smile.

"You know, that's the best advice I've heard." Morgan nodded. "I probably should have told her not to fix me up in the first place. But she insists that I need to date." She laughed. "What I need is a psychiatrist to tell me why I would agree to such torture."

Mr. Johnson laughed with her. At least she was glad to know that she hadn't lost her ability to laugh.

She watched Mr. Johnson's face go through a range of comical expressions and she wondered why.

"Mr. Johnson, what are you thinking about?"

"You," he chuckled. "You young folks. I think you're just having a bad spell. But you keep on trying. I know you're gonna find your prince charming. Hold out for that hero." He rubbed her hand. "Trust me on this, I know you're gonna find your hero, and when you do, you have to name your first born Duke."

The pair laughed loudly. After a few moments, Morgan sobered. "Sure, I'll find my hero." Even though a part of her was skeptical.

"Miss Morgan?" Mr. Johnson interrupted her thoughts. "Can I ask you a question?"

She looked at him. "Sure, you can." She held her breath.

He cleared his throat and leaned close to her ear. "What kind of man are you looking for?"

"You know, Mr. Johnson, I'm not sure. I think once I answer that question, I may be home free. Actually, to be honest, I really don't have the time for a relationship. I mean, the business keeps me so busy I barely have enough time to eat."

"That might be just an excuse." He leaned back and looked her in the eyes. "But you young folks know more than us old folks." He tapped her hand and smiled. "I'll be right back." He slipped from the barstool.

Morgan gave a lot of thought to his question. What was she looking for in a man? Traits came rolling forward. She grabbed a napkin from the table behind her, pulled a pen from her purse and began scribbling. She listed honesty first, followed by faithfulness, integrity, self confidence, self-love, fearlessness and lastly, sensuality. She looked at her list and nodded her head. Yes, this was what she was looking for, but hadn't ever sat down and put it down in black in white. Now that she had, her next task was to halt Yavette and her matchmaking tactics. True, she had agreed to three blind dates, and it seemed as if number two was going to stand her up. She looked around and noticed no one in the bar remotely fitting Tony's description. Yet, for some reason, she felt relieved, not angry about being stood up. As she rose from her seat, Mr. Johnson returned.

"Leaving so soon?"

"Yeah, this guy isn't going to show, and I've got some work I could tend to. Besides, I hadn't planned on staying out all evening. I have to go to work in the morning." Morgan pulled a twenty out of her purse. "If I stay here all night, I won't get anything done."

"Won't you at least dance with me one time? It is Steppers Night." His eyes begged.

Morgan looked at him, then smiled. "Okay. Just one, and then I really have to go."

One dance turned into ten as she and Mr. Johnson danced to several steppers' songs. After nearly an hour of them twirling and stepping, Morgan found herself dragging Mr. Johnson from the dance floor. She had noticed several times while they danced that he kept looking toward the entrance, as if he were expecting someone.

"Mr. Johnson, I really have to go."

"Aww, just one more dance." He smiled and looked toward the door.

"I'd love to, but I've got to get some sleep." She kissed Mr. Johnson on the cheek and warmed at the softness of it. To her, Mr. Johnson was more like an uncle than the playa-playa he tried to make himself out to be. "But I've had a great time tonight. We'll have to do this again."

"You sure you gotta go?"

"I'm sure, Mr. Johnson." Morgan headed toward the exit.

"Wait," he walked her to the exit. "Don't forget what I asked you. Okay? And I don't think you're crazy. You just haven't found the right man. He's gonna walk through that door. Mark my words."

"I will, Mr. Johnson. Thank you for listening." She waved over her head and exited the bar.

"Nick, what took you so long? I called you over an hour ago!"

"I got here as soon as possible. I had to stop at Dad's first. What's wrong?"

Mr. Johnson rose from his feet and stood nearly chest to chest with Nick. "Damn, you'd think you were riding in a horse and buggy, it took you so long. Your daddy only lives ten miles from here." Mr. Johnson waved his hand in dismissal. "Never mind, now. I don't need you. She's gone."

"Who?"

"Aww, you young folks." Mr. Johnson downed his drink and stormed out of the bar.

Nick watched Mr. Johnson's retreating back. He spun around when he got a whiff of that intoxicating fragrance that held his senses in a vicious grip. He looked around the bar, but he didn't see her. He wondered if Mr. Johnson wastalking about Morgan.

"Hey, Nick," a female voice purred. "Long time."

Nick didn't want to face the voice he knew so well, one that had called out his name many a nights. He steeled himself then turned.

"Hi, Sheila. How've you been?"

"Great. And I see you and this place are doing well."

Nick nodded his head and looked her in the eye. *Still beautiful and up to no good,* he thought as he looked into her grey eyes, made so by the colored contacts. He noticed she had colored her hair a wild honey-blonde, which he had to admit was a crazed contrast to her deep brown complexion. Yet, she was still built like a brick house—her large bosom overshadowed her small waist and ample hips.

"We were in the neighborhood and thought we'd drop by and see the new remodeling."

He raised his eyebrows at "we," then spotted the object of her noun.

"Nick, this is my husband, Donald. Don, this is Nick, my ex-fiancé and the owner of this fine establishment."

He heard the unmistakable sarcastic dig at his bar. If she had been a man, he'd havephysically escorted her out. Instead, he placed his hand out to her husband and watched as he reluctantly accepted the gesture.

"Well, welcome to Nick's. Find yourselves a seat and your drinks are on me tonight."

Nick smiled painfully and walked away. What on God's green earth had called for him to make such a generous offer to the woman who had practically spat on his dreams? Thoughts of Morgan, and how she had whirled into his bar and seeped into his very being, came to him. He looked for David.

"Hey, what are you doing here so early?" David asked as he came from the stockroom.

"Mr. Johnson called me." Nick took a case a beer from atop a case of rum.

"Oh, yeah, he and Morgan were here. She's fine, dude. You're lucky I'm married."

"She was here?!"

"Yup. She and Mr. Johnson danced part of the night away. Too bad you weren't here. You could have given that sister your phone number." David nodded his head and began stocking the cooler with the beer.

"Damn, what gives?" Nick said out loud, then shook his head from side to side.

He wondered if he would ever get the chance. "Well, this can't get any stranger, but Shelia and her husband just walked in."

David straightened and looked in the direction Nick tilted his head toward. They both watched as Sheila and her husband stepped over to a small table made for two. He noticed the animated way in which she fawned and cooed over her latest attraction. He shook his head and headed to the rear office. After a few words with Elena, who was training a new bar maid, and then David, promising to return to close, he left. As he headed for the door, he turned to see Sheila and her husband dancing on the dance floor. He smirked at the wicked smile on her face, a smile that at one time would have had him drooling and crawling. Now, it meant nothing. He smiled back and left the bar, and the last of his thoughts of Sheila, behind.

The cell phone in his pocket rang. He pulled it out and looked at the caller ID. He began to laugh.

"What's up, Jack?"

"You, man. I called the crib."

"I'm just leaving the bar. What's up?"

"Did you send the basket?"

"Sure did, and it seems as if her blind date stood her up. She just left. I didn't get a chance to see her, but David said she was at the bar dancing with Mr. Johnson."

"Old Man Johnson?"

Nick chuckled. "The one and only."

"Dude, you better act fast. Old Man Johnson is an original pimp."

The pair laughed before Nick became somber. "I'm trying, Jack. Every time I get an opportunity, something gets in the way. Hell, I'm beginning to think that there are forces out there that want to keep us apart."

"Don't give up yet. Besides, there's the card party next week."

"She needs to know me before that, Jack. I don't want to spring all this on her at the party. Are you crazy?"

"Hey, hey! Don't get testy with me. Look I gotta run, we just wanted to know if you sent the basket."

"Yes. And if you're wondering, I signed it N. J. Chambers, Jr. And tell Yavette, no more blind dates!"

He heard Jackson chuckle. "Sure thing, Casanova. I'll talk to you later."

"Later." Nick disconnected the call then tossed the phone onto the passenger seat. As he headed toward home, he wondered, for the umpteenth time that day, what was Morgan up to and how she would receive him once he told her the truth. He'd hoped that she would accept him and his reason for not telling her the entire truth up front. He needed something to sooth the dull ache. A taste of ice cream should do it. He rounded the block to head toward Rainbow Ice Cream Shop on Western Avenue.

CHAPTER 12

Morgan stood at the counter and scanned the board that listed over 100 different flavors of ice cream.. She loved ice cream, no matter the weather outside. And on this night, with the two crazed blind dates behind her and one that stood her up, her body would be satiated by nothing less than a double scoop sundae with butter pecan ice cream, marshmallow topping, nuts and cherries.

"I'll take a banana split, chocolate almond ice cream, extra nuts and cherries."

Morgan heard the voice, bent slightly at the waist and looked to her left. Three people down stood Jarrod. Unbelievable, she thought as she looked at the brother whose chocolate-chip face and those cute, deep dimples wouldn't leave her mind. She straightened and prayed that the warmth rising from her neck would not cause her to break out into an all encompassing, drenching sweat.

"Here ya go, ma'am. That will be three dollars and seventy-four cents," said the cashier.

"Add hers to mine," Nick said as he stood next to her and handed the cashier two five-dollar bills. Morgan looked up and smiled. She let her eyes trail down the arm, clad in a black suede jacket; a white turtle-neck peeked from under it. She wanted to faint. He looked too damn good, the white a wicked contrast to his beautiful complexion.

"Thank you, Jarrod. I see you know good ice cream."

"This is one of my favorite joints. Baskin Robbins is good, and Cold Stone ain't bad, but the variety here can't be beat. You live around here?"

"No, I live in the Oakwood community, but I grew up not too far from here. What about you?"

"I don't live too far from here."

They stood near each, neither knowing what to say next. He didn't believe in happenstance. He knew, felt deep in his gut, that everything happens for a reason.

"Umm, are you going to take your sundae with you or are you going to eat here?"

"I was going to take it out," Morgan replied, then quickly changed her mind at the brief look of disappointment in his eyes. "But if you're staying, and don't mind the company, then I'll eat mine here."

Nick smiled. "I have a better idea. Let's sit in my truck." He grabbed their bags filled with their treats, took Morgan by the elbow and escorted her to his truck. After depressing the remote, he opened the passenger door and assisted her into the SUV. He shut the door and steeled himself from running around to the driver's side.

Morgan held the cell phone she had sat on in her hand and looked around the leather interior. She wondered how a simple bartender could afford a Mercedes SUV. Naw, she couldn't see him dealing anything other than drinks legally, but still, how could he afford such an extravagance on what he probably made as a bartender. *Heck,* she mused silently, *he couldn't make over thirty grand.*

He looked at her hands as she held his cell phone. She seemed deep in thought.

"Thanks," he interrupted her and took the cell from her hand. He wanted to toss it in the back seat, in case it became a distraction, but knew that he needed to keep it near in case David had an emergency at the bar. Instead, he placed the cell phone into its holder attached to his hip on the left.

They sat and ate their ice cream and talked about growing up in Chicago, and the schools they attended, including college. As he talked, Morgan could see that Jarrod was super intelligent, and wondered why he didn't own his own business, versus working for someone else.

As their conversation segued into religion, of which Morgan told Jarrod that her father was a minister, Jarrod admitted to his near miss with marriage.

"Don't get me wrong, I want to get married, but we have to be compatible," Jarrod said, and looked at Morgan.

She wished she could see his eyes, because something in his stare made her sit up and take notice. She'd been married before, and she wasn't sure she wanted to roll down that aisle again.

She looked at him as the conversation took another turn about dates. Morgan tried to relax. She remembered having told Jarrod when she first started coming to Nick's about her striking out with dates, now she wasn't so sure she wanted to tell him about her resorting to dates from the Internet and the blind dates. Yet she laughed when Jarrod began to talk about his last blind date who threw a brick through his window.

Morgan began to relax. Fortunately, she hadn't broken out into a sweat, but she could feel slight moisture above her lip when he asked her what she did for a living. She told him, leaving out the part of her being owner and president.

"Wow, sounds interesting."

"It can be. But let me not bore you." She looked at the clock on the console. It was nearly 10 o'clock. "Do let me thank you, though. For the second time tonight I've had a great time."

He looked at her. "Second?"

"Yeah, I was at Nick's tonight. Me and Mr. Johnson danced for hours. He didn't want me to leave." She chuckled. "He's something else. Like an old uncle."

"Yeah, that he is." *So, that's why he wanted me to come to the bar,* Nick realized. *He wanted me to see Morgan.*

Nick looked at her and noticed her twists hanging about her shoulders, slightly shielding her face, the scent of that wicked perfume. He wanted to kiss her, wanted to taste her lips—see if they were as soft as they appeared. His eyes narrowed as his body began to betray him. Embarrassed, he shifted in his seat, grateful for the dark interior. He had no intentions of jumping her like some teenager with raging hormones. Yet, he wondered what the hell was wrong with him. He hadn't reacted like a randy boy in…well, never.

They spoke at the same time.

"No, ladies first."

"No, I interrupted you. What were you going to say?" she looked up at him.

"I want to show you something. And I have something I've been meaning to tell you for some time." He looked at her, and noticed the guarded look in her eyes. "Trust me, Morgan. Will you ride with me to Indianapolis Boulevard in Indiana?"

Morgan tilted her head. Even she had to admit that she wasn't quite ready for this impromptu date to end. She was enjoying his company and wanted to hear his deep voice over and over again, feel the tingling sensation rise from her feet to her scalp. And those dimples when he smiled. She couldn't seem to get him out of her senses, out of her mind.

"Okay. I'll go," Morgan said as she watched Jarrod start the vehicle and put it in gear. She settled back into the comfort of the leather seats while Jarrod searched for a radio station before he adjusted the volume of the radio from controls on the steering wheel.

As she rode, Jarrod began talking about his two brothers, Nehemiah and David, the death of his mother and how he came to be at Nick's. As he crossed the Illinois border leading into Indiana, he told how he had worked as a financial analyst, working part time in the bar.

She looked at his proud profile as he came to stop at what looked like was once a drive-in theatre. He pulled up to a large fence, reached across her lap to the glove compartment, and retrieved a set of keys. "Sit tight. I'll be right back," he said as he stepped from the vehicle.

Rapt curiosity claimed her as she watched him unlock the gate. She began to wonder just who Jarrod was to have keys to an abandoned drive-in.

"Don't worry," he said as he climbed back behind the wheel. "I'm no trespasser, but I wanted to show you this." He drove past the fence, hopped out, closed the fence, and then returned to the vehicle. He drove across the gravel landscape and surreptitiously spied her from the corner of his eye. He wondered what she was thinking.

He stopped near the center of the large area and parked. He shut off the engine, but not the radio, as he opened the moon roof to allow the view of the full moon and stars shine in. He leaned his seat back and smiled when he caught Morgan openly observing him. If he didn't know any better, he'd sworn she was staring at his lips.

Morgan placed her hands in her lap. She had watched him, his fluid movements, the way his lips stretched just right across his even teeth, the dimples when he smiled. *Lord, this man is sexy!* She tempered her thoughts.

He turned in his seat and watched Morgan as the look in her eyes changed from guarded to curiosity to sensuality. He had to get them out of the close confines of the vehicle before he did something crazy like pulling her to him and kissing her, letting his lips fall upon hers.

"Would you like to step out?" He rolled down the windows.

She nodded and made motion to move. He chuckled as he reached over her and unbuckled her seat belt. "Hold tight." He tapped her arm.

Morgan watched as he rounded the vehicle to the passenger side. He opened the door and put his hand out for her to grasp. She placed her small hand in his larger one and felt the strength of his hands as he helped her from the SUV. He held her hand and stood over her. He looked into her eyes then took a deep breath.

"Morgan. I own this lot, a day spa in Lake Geneva, a few investment properties and Nick's."

Morgan turned her head to the side. "What did you say?"

He cleared his throat. "My name is Nicholas Jarrod Chambers, Jr. My family and friends call me Nicky. And I'm the owner of Nick's Sports Bar and Grille."

Blinking her eyes several times, she looked into his eyes and saw the apprehension in them. "Wow!" was all she could say. She stepped to the side and walked toward the front of the SUV. She looked him up and down, taking in the high grain suede jacket and the highly polished loafers on his feet. She wasn't angry, not in the least, but she knew it was time for her to be honest as well.

"Are you mad at me for not telling you sooner?"

"Oh, my no." She walked back over to where he stood and stepped in front of him. "My turn." She held her head up high. "My full name is Morgan Marie Paige, proud owner of Paige Public Relations."

For a long moment, the two stared at each other, realization hitting them both.

Suddenly, they began to laugh loudly just before they embraced.

"Okay, now tell me why you didn't tell me all those times you came to the bar about owning a business."

"Probably the same reasons you have. I want people to like me for me, not because I own a company whose client roster includes some great professional athletes. My clients give me tickets to all sorts of playoff events." She shrugged her shoulders, then folded her arms. "Why didn't you tell me?"

"Like you said, plus, initially I didn't think that it mattered all that much. But later ..." his voice trailed off.

"Later?" she whispered.

"Well, I've liked you from the moment you walked into the bar. And I almost asked you out that last night I saw you before I closed the bar for renovations. I wanted to kick myself because I let you get away and didn't get your number. But then you walked in for the re-opening night, and I knew I wasn't going to let another opportunity pass to get to know you better."

"Wait! Your initials: NJC, Jr. You sent the basket of flowers today, didn't you?"

She watched as he nodded his head.

"How did you get my address?"

He looked away. Time to come completely clean. "My best friend, Jackson, is engaged to your cousin, Yavette."

"No way!" She exclaimed loudly. "You're the best friend that she was talking about setting me up with." She watched as he nodded his head up and down. "This is unreal."

"Are you ready? 'Cause there's more?"

Steeling herself, she felt she had a clue as to what he was going to say next. She looked up at him. "Go ahead."

"I'm your final blind date."

"I'm going to kill Yavette." She laughed. "And she wasn't going to tell me."

"I asked her not to. But we're here and talking, and I didn't want to wait until the party."

Relief flooded Morgan. He had not only saved her from having to ask him out, but she had just been rescued from having to tell Yavette that there would be no third blind date. She smiled broadly.

"What did I do?"

"Do?" She responded.

"Yes. What did I do to bring on that beautiful smile of yours? Tell me, and I'll do it again."

Morgan blushed, then felt his hand gently touch her chin, forcing her to meet his stare dead on. "Tell me what I have to do to get you to agree to go out with me." His face came closer and Morgan closed her eyes as she felt the tingling start in her scalp and shimmy its way down to her toes. She wanted to sink to the ground when his lips touched hers—the feel of the softness of his full lips on hers shook her. She felt his large arms surround her and pull her closer.

He released her. "Morgan." He called her name. "Tell me, baby. What do I have to do?"

She wasn't sure she'd find her voice, she thought as she opened her eyes. She could see that he was serious and was waiting for her to answer him. "All you have to do is ask," she responded as she put her hands up to his cheeks and nudged him closer. She closed her eyes again as her lips met his. She sighed when he ended the kiss.

"How old are you, Morgan?"

"I'm thirty-two. How old are you?"

"Thirty-nine. And feel free to call me Nick or Nicky." He pulled her into his arms and began swaying side to side as a slow song seeped from the speakers inside the car. The slight feel of her full breasts against the lower half of his chest singed him. He hoped the erection wouldn't rise, that his coat would shield him, keep him from being embarrassed. He didn't want her to bolt, for he wasn't looking for a hit and run. He wanted to get to know her.

"Morgan, will you go out with me?" He asked and looked down into her upturned face. She nodded, then laid her head back on his chest.

Morgan could hear the beating of his heart, felt it through his turtleneck sweater. She inhaled deeply the pure masculine scent of him mixed with an exotic cologne that caused her senses to overload. The mixture was proving to be some sort of aphrodisiac. One that Morgan was beginning to feel powerless to resist.

Their motions were slow and sure as they held on to each other—Morgan's arms around his wide back, Nick's arms wrapped around her waist.

Simultaneously, they looked at each other. She stared into his eyes, a deep darkness had claimed the light color, adding a depth of sensuality to them, making Morgan shiver. His face began to fade again as his head bent and his lips touched hers. She moaned at the electric sensation the innocent move elicited from her. Without shame, Morgan placed her hands about his head and began to nibble at his full lips. Nick met her, forcing her lips to part to feast on her tongue.

One or the other moaned loudly as the act intensified. Morgan stroked the side of his smooth face. Her fingers touched and lightly caressed his skin. He pulled her closer, allowing her to felt he full extent of what her ministrations were doing to him. God forbid she touched his bare body—he'd be lost for sure.

Nick broke the kiss and stared down at her. He watched as her chest rose and fell, and he wanted to feel them rise and fall against his face, his lips lavishing her chest, tongue plying her flesh. He could see the uncertainty mixed with pure need in her eyes. She looked vulnerable. The last thing he wanted to do was scare her, but Lord she had made him need, made him want her with just a touch of her fingers. He cleared his throat. "Let's get out of here."

"Baby, come here," she heard him call out to her. She watched the intensity in his eyes as she slowly walked toward him. The music in his head was nothing compared to the vicious tune her ample hips were playing as she moved gracefully toward him. She stopped two feet in front of him and bent over slightly, poking her lips out. He laughed as he met her, closing the space between them and pulled her into his arms. Morgan went slack in his strong arms as his lips met hers, forcing them open to receive his tongue.

She moaned from deep in her throat. She had never wanted any man the way she wanted Jarrod. She wanted to see him—to feel the weight of him on her—to have him hold her to him—make her safe.

He broke the kiss and allowed his eyes to speak to her, to send the message that he wanted her, wanted to lay her on this bed and make love to her.

One part of her wanted to deny him, while the other chided her and made her bold and brazen. She knew from the look on his face that he wouldn't, couldn't let her go—he had to have her. She sighed loudly, as he pulled her into his arms, then she heard him chuckled as he backed her up to the wall, her hands splayed across it.

Jarrod stepped closer to Morgan, the shape of her full breasts were mere inches from his chest. He leaned down and kissed her forehead, followed by her pert nose, the sides of her face and cheeks, down her neck. When she shivered, he knew he had hit at least one spot. He decided to explore further as his lips met hers, softly at first as he held her face in his large hands. They both heard the deep, throaty moan escape her—his kiss intensified as his tongue began to mate with hers.

Morgan broke the kiss and looked up at him. She knew she was breathing hard, her breath came out in short pants. His eyes had turned dark with desire, and she was sure hers matched his. Never had a kiss been so erotic and electric all at the same time. Her eyes went to his full lips. She pulled his face to hers and rained kisses across his eyelids as her hands moved from the softness of his smooth head, to slowly move up and down his back. She wanted to feel him. Wanted the barrier between them removed. She began kissing his lips—soft pecks at first.

When she licked his lips, then lightly parted them, he groaned loudly much to Morgan's undoing. The sound was like music to her ears—the prodding she needed.

Morgan moved from his embrace, stepped back and began to slowly undress. She watched him as his eyes became mere slats to peer from. As she reached around to unhook her bra, letting the flimsy garment fall to the floor, she smiled slightly when he closed his eyes and pushed himself from the bed.

"Allow me to finish," he breathed heavily as his mouth covered a nipple, worrying it to a torrid peak and causing Morgan's legs to tremble. He left her breast and swiftly picked her up into his arms. He laid her on the center of the bed and looked languidly at her as she lay there, dressed only in a pair of wicked red panties.

Taking his fingers, he made a path down the center of her chest to the area just above her bud. She shut her eyes and arched her back as his fingers teased the bud, coaxing it to life, causing the bud to throb as her hips met his fingers. The sensation proved too much as the first orgasm bubbled at the surface. No. Morgan didn't want that—didn't want him to see her as her body began to betray her mind.

"Give me all of you, Morgan," he said as his fingers moved with more intensity. "Don't hold back on me, baby. Look at me. I want all of you."

Morgan opened her eyes and saw the look—one she recognized, but didn't want to believe. She saw love in his eyes.

She began to whimper. Tears threatened to fall from her eyes. He wouldn't let up—wouldn't stop until he knew she had the release, was more than ready for what he had to offer her. Morgan grabbed a handful of bed covers and exploded, her eyes focused on Jarrod's as he continued to stroke her through the end of the orgasm.

"Are you ready?"

Her legs trembled and her bud throbbed.

In one swift motion, Jarrod had removed his own clothing, retrieved a condom, then positioned himself over her. "I've wanted to make love to you ever since I laid eyes on you."

Morgan couldn't speak as she felt him at her apex, the beginning of him, the very thing that made him man teased her. As he inched forward, Morgan moved her hips forward, her eyes shut. He moved back. He wanted her hear her. Wanted her to tell him she wanted him as much as he wanted her. And though the mere gesture was about to become his undoing, he was intent on having Morgan reach out to him.

"Are you ready, baby?"

Morgan nodded her head and moved her hips again, just as he sank in a little more. She wanted to scream.

"Baby, are you sure, you're ready?" he whispered as he moved another centimeter.

She opened her eyes and trembled at the dark desire. In all of her adult life, she had never wanted to love a man like she wanted to love Jarrod. She was more than ready, but was he?

"Yes, Jarrod, I'm ready!"

In one motion, he filled her. They both shuddered at the intense emotion, feeling of being in each other's arms, their bodies as one. He didn't want to move. Didn't want to end the beginning of the sweetest feeling he had ever known. As he laid atop his dream, her arms wrapped around him, her fingers stroking him, his arms around her, supporting their weight, his heart tugged, and he was stunned at the deep emotion. He looked at her and knew that after tonight, they would forever be a part of the other—that she had given him a gift, one that would remain with him for the rest of his life. And that scared him. Yet he wanted her and here she was.

Morgan saw the odd look on his face. She wondered about it briefly as he began to move inside of her, his girth sheathed within her tightness. She wanted more of him. Wanted to feel him deep in her soul, to touch that place within.

They moved together, the sensations crept up each and wound them up, pulling then pushing them toward the release, one that neither wanted to come yet, while they both secretly wished to experience over and again.

Morgan opened her legs wider and snaked them around Jarrod's waist. He moved deeper and groaned, the sensation of her body close to his, the warmth of her hands caressing him, the wicked feel of her tightness that held him as a sweet captor, was too much. He pulled her closer, their rhythm increased as the crescendo peaked. Jarrod let out a loud groan as he felt her tighten around him, the sensation too great to ignore and much too intense to hold back, but he wanted to wait. Wanted to feel her release, hear her moan his name. As if she'd read his mind, Morgan began to quiver, her apex tightened around Jarrod's manhood, and she moaned out his name. That was Jarrod's undoing, as he joined her moments later.

As he rolled over to one side, he pulled her with him to rest on top of him. He never wanted to let her go, and knew the three words that would make her stay, make her want to forever be his.

"Morgan, I love you."

CHAPTER 13

Morgan sat up with a start. Her chest heaved up and down, and she was sweating profusely, her twists were plastered to the side of her face. She touched her bare bottom and felt wetness—her own.

"That was deep," she mumbled as she began to remember the wholly erotic dream of her making love with Nick. "Oh, my gosh," she breathed out as she tried to remember the last time she had had a wet dream. She couldn't recall ever having one as intense as the one she'd just had.

She looked over at the clock. The dial read 3 A.M. She had to take a quick shower.

As she lathered her body with her favorite scented shower gel, she smiled at the thought of her unexpected night with Nick, the man she once called Jarrod. As they embraced at the vacant drive-in, her lips on his, he had gotten an urgent call from his brother. As he drove her back to her car, he held her hand in his. Once at her car, he insisted that she call him once she arrived home and had given her all his phone numbers: home, cell, bar. She smiled as she looked at all the numbers. He then flipped out a business card and asked for her number. She did likewise and gave him all of her numbers.

When she had arrived home, Morgan could hear the phone ringing from outside her condo. She quickly unlocked the door. It could be Nick, she thought. She rushed to the phone in her den, Patton and Davis close on her heels, and looked down at the caller ID unit on her desk just as she reached out her hand to pick up the receiver.

"Oh, no I won't." She pulled back her hand and shook her head. The caller ID listed Thomas's name. She flipped her fingers and turned her nose up. He was the last person she wanted to talk to. She knew who she wanted to talk to.

She had turned on some music. The sweet melodic tune of Barry White flowed out of the overhead Bose speakers situated in each room. Morgan dialed Nick's cell number. A smile eased across her face when she heard his voice on the other end. They spoke for a few moments, his telling her that a pipe burst in the boiler room and had caused the room to flood. As they were about to ring off, Nick told her to free up her evening Saturday. She agreed, then bid him a good night before she disconnected the call.

After her shower, Morgan grinned as she thought of Nick's smooth voice, the way his hand felt on the small of her waist, the way his eyes shone in the semi-darkness of the parking lot as they sat and talked, then later as they slow danced. For all the dates she'd had, she had never had one so engaging, one that awakened every nerve she had in her body.

As she climbed back into bed, Morgan knew she would have to call off the next date and made a mental note to call Yavette first thing in the morning to do just that. Besides, she said to herself, Tony is out to lunch—Nick is definitely over for dinner.

Her mind wandered in and out of images of him: his wonderful smile, those sweet dimples, and them hypnotic eyes! If she didn't know any better, she'd say the man had put her under a spell for the dream was too real. And if that was the case, it was one spell she didn't want to come from under any time soon.

Nick woke to the jangling sound of the phone. He grumbled as he rolled over and picked up the caller-ID unit. With one eye open, he spied the words "private." He picked up the entire phone, flipped it over, shut off the ringer, then placed the phone back on the nightstand. He flopped onto his back and rested his forearm over his face. A few more hours of sleep and he'd be lucent. Any less, he'd be grouchy as a hungry bear for the rest of the day. He wasn't due to go to the bar until six that evening.

After several hours, Nick rose and began his day. He returned several phone calls, of which two were from his brothers. He had listened as David droned on about his job, his wife Miranda and an upcoming Bulls game, of which he had four front row seats. Nick agreed to attend, rang off, then called Nehemiah.

"How was your evening?"

"Man, it was great. I went out with Morgan's girl."

"Really? I didn't know you had a date."

"Yeah, and she's a real sweet woman. By the way, I was just wondering, are you Nick yet? Or are you still Jarrod?" Nehemiah laughed. "Man, at first I agreed with you, but now, after talking to Tina, I don't think you should hold out telling Morgan who you really are."

"I did."

"You did what? You told her the truth?"

"Yup. We had a little unexpected meeting last night, and I got a chance to tell her. Why do you want to know?"

"Man, I told Tina all about you."

Nick rolled his eyes upward. Thank God he told her. He vaguely remembered the woman with Morgan. The fit of Morgan's jeans and the playful smile on her face as she danced that night away stole his attention. Admittedly, he hadn't liked watching her dance with those guys, but at least she hadn't slow danced with any of them, letting some strange dude pull her close and hold her tight. *He* wanted to be the only one to take her into his arms and hold her close, just like he had at the vacant drive-in.

"Nick? You still there?"

"Yeah, what?"

"I asked you a question."

"Okay, what?"

Nehemiah laughed. "You got it bad, brother. But I do understand. She should have been arrested for wearing those jeans."

"Hey!" Nick barked into the phone, then chuckled. "Keep your eyes on her friend."

"I plan to do just that. We're going out again on Sunday."

"Oh really? And what about your home situation?"

"What about it?"

"Man, don't do this."

"Do what, Nick?"

Nick signed loudly into the phone. He couldn't believe that his brother was going to jump right back into playing crazy mind games with women. Hadn't Cara been enough?

"You didn't answer me, Nick. Do what?" he replied, his voice a low growl.

"You know. Play stupid pet tricks with women."

"Naw, Nick, I've had enough games to last me a life time. I like Tina. I liked what I heard and saw."

Nick was relieved to hear his brother admit, for once, that the head games were tiring, yet he still wasn't convinced that he was over Cara and ready to move forward with someone else.

"Don't you think it's too soon? I mean, you and Cara aren't even divorced. And what about setting aside a little time to get your head right?"

"My head is more right today than it has been in a long time." Nehemiah let out a loud sigh. "I'll admit it. I didn't love Cara. We were two peas in a pod. I wanted to change her, and she wanted to change me. Like Tina said, 'You can't change people, make them over into what you think is great.' "

"Okay, brother. I'm just checking. No need for the sister to get into any of your madness."

Nehemiah chuckled sourly. "Yeah, I hear ya. Hey, I need a big favor."

"What do you need?"

"I need a place to crash until I get on my feet. You know I don't want to stay with David and Miranda, them looking at me like I done lost my friend Flicker. And I don't want to stay another night with

Dad. He shakes his head every time he looks my way, like I've fallen off a wagon and hit my freakin' head."

Nick laughed. He knew their father's looks. "Sure, you can stay with me. You either can take one of the spare rooms upstairs, or you can camp out in the basement. But there's only one rule in this house. You move it, you put it back the way you got it. Other than that, *mi casa es su casa*."

"Thanks. I'll move my stuff tomorrow."

Nick talked to Nehemiah for an additional half hour before he got ready for another night at Nick's Bar and Grille. As he dressed in a pair of jeans and the signature jersey with the bar's name across it, he thought how his night could improve with a visit from Morgan.

Nick looked into the mirror attached to his closet. He looked around his room, then back to his image. He opened the closet door, pulled out a pair of dress olive slacks, a pale Lowden colored, collarless, pullover silk shirt and a mustard gold wool blazer. Quickly, he stripped to his black boxers and T-shirt and put on the dressier attire. Nick fished around the bottom of his closet and found the deep olive cap toe shoes. He removed the dark, thick athletic socks and replaced them with a pair of dressier olive colored socks, with flecks of gold. He put on his shoes, stole one last glance in the mirror. Pleased with what he saw, he grabbed his wallet and keys and headed for the door.

He stopped when he spotted the bottle of cologne sitting on his bureau. He placed his keys and wallet down, pulled his shirt from his pants. He quickly shook some of the liquid into the palms of his hand. He rubbed his hands together then over his chest, up to his neck, then across the top of his head. He sniffed the air around him. He smiled as he nodded. He grabbed his stuff and rushed toward his SUV.

He hadn't spoken with Morgan to find out if she was coming to the bar, but he was prepared to leave and go to her—show her another facet of Nicholas Jarrod Chambers, Jr.

Friday had come too quickly for Morgan. She was tired and knew that she should stay in and rest, yet, for some inexplicable reason, she was fidgety and couldn't quite settle down enough to fully relax. She had enjoyed her entire week, even the crazed press conference with Willie, yet the week had been made even more so with the impromptu date with Nick.

She padded on bare feet into her home office and sat down at her computer. She opened her email and frowned when she noticed she had several from LawMan1. She deleted them all.

As she continued to scan her email, the phone on the desk began to ring. She looked at the caller ID, then picked up the receiver.

"Hey, Tina."

"Morning, Boss Lady. Are you coming in today?"

Morgan looked at the clock. By this hour she would have already been at the office. "Yeah, I'll be in later. I had a late night. So, how was your date?"

Morgan listened as Tina went on about her date with Nehemiah, and how they spent the night together.

"Wait, don't think like that. We didn't do anything. We were watching an old movie and I fell asleep with my head on his thigh. When I woke up this morning, we were holding each other. But I've got something to tell you."

She had an idea what Tina wanted to say. If she knew people right, they got to discussing their lives and Nehemiah told her who owns Nick's. "Can I guess?"

"Morgan, this is serious."

"Come on, let me guess. Nick's Bar and Grille is owned by Nicholas Jarrod Chambers, Jr., Nehemiah's younger brother."

"How did you know that?"

Morgan told Tina about their unplanned date. They both chuckled. "Well, I'm glad you know, but I knew he had a thing for you. I saw it in the way he paid attention to you—seemed to cater just to you. And that's what you need, a brother to take care of you, protect you. You don't need no brother who's afraid to step out there and take some risks—both personally and professionally."

She could only nod her head as she listened to Tina. After a half hour, the pair rang off, and Morgan decided to head into the office.

Two hours later, as she got ready to leave, her phone began to ring. She rushed to the kitchen and looked at the caller-ID on the cordless. She smiled as the unit displayed a portion of the name of the man from her wicked dream: Nick's Sports Bar.

"Hello," she said.

"Hey, you. How are you?"

Morgan sat down on the couch. "I'm well. About to go into the office for a few hours. How are you?"

"Good. At the bar working on a few invoices. I've been thinking about you."

She blushed. "Really. What have you been thinking about?"

"Spending the few days hanging out with you—getting to know you. Are you game?"

"What about the bar?"

"I've got a few good people to take care of it. It'll keep. Besides, I have the cell if they need me, like last night."

"What do you have in mind?"

"Allow me to cook you dinner at my place. Tonight."

"What can you cook?"

"A mean bowl of fried corn flakes!" Nick laughed. He sobered. "Now, Miss Morgan, would I offer to cook you dinner and not try and show off my culinary skills?"

"Brotha man, you might." She responded playfully, then looked out the window at the grey day and thought that this type of day was made for snuggling. She scooted over as her two pets posted themselves alongside her on the couch.

"No, I wouldn't. And I'll sweeten the pot. How about I pick you up?"

"Whoa. All this sounds tempting." Her smiled widened at the deep timbre of his voice.

"Is it tempting enough to get you to say yes?"

"Yes," she replied and gave him her address.

"Great. How about I pick you up at seven?"

"Sounds good. I'll be ready. Should I prepare a desert? Bring a bottle of wine?"

"Nope, just be ready to be well fed. And I hope you like old movies."

"As a matter of fact, I do."

"What's your favorite?" he asked.

"All This, and Heaven Too."

"Aww, that's a classic. Circa 1940 with Charles Boyer. Got an Academy Award nomination that year for Best Picture."

"What about you? What's your favorite?" She laid back on the couch and began to twirl a twist around her finger.

"Key Largo."

"Good choice, but just about anything with Humphrey Bogart pre 1950 was great! My favorite was the Maltese Falcon, 1948, with his wife, Lauren Bacall."

Morgan and Nick continued to speak on the phone, laughing and sharing more about themselves. Both were surprised to learn that they shared the same tastes in books, movies and music.

"Nicholas Jarrod, I've gotta get off this phone. I could talk to you for hours, but I really need to go to the office for at least a few hours, and already it's going on two."

"Awright, baby, I'll let you go, and I'll see you at seven. Bye."

"Looking forward to it. Bye-bye." She placed the cordless phone on the coffee table.

Morgan rushed out of her condo and headed to her office. She tried to focus, but her mind wouldn't concentrate on anything but Nick. She had to admit that she was excited about seeing him again. An emotion she hadn't felt in a long time lodged itself in her chest. She really liked Nick, but she also didn't want to go too fast, didn't want to wake up, like she did with Michael, and no longer like Nick.

Tina appeared in the doorway. "Yavette is on the phone."

"Thanks." Morgan picked up the phone. "Hey, girl, what's up?"

"Nothing. What's up with you?"

"Not a thing. Why do you ask?"

"Well, I thought I'd a heard from you by now about your date with Tony."

"Aww, that dude stood me up." Morgan knew her voice didn't hold a trace of disappointment.

"Damn, what gives with the brothers?"

"I don't know, but it's time for you to give up the whole match making scheme and admit that you can't match me. I'm fine. I'm okay."

"No, it's not. I've got the perfect date. You said three—agreed to three."

"I'll agree to a lobotomy if I'm foolish enough to let you set me up on another one."

"Hey, word is bond. You said three, and I've the perfect date. I told you that Jackson has a best friend, good looking guy, who I think would be perfect for you."

Morgan shook her head and wondered if Yavette would tell her the truth—let her in on the secret she was harboring.

"What's this guy's name?"

"Umm, I want you to meet him without exchanging names. You'll meet at the party. And if you don't like each other, then you aren't tied up together anywhere with no way out. Umm, he doesn't know your name, either."

No, Morgan's mind screamed, she's going to keep this one close and she lied!

Unbelievable. Her own cousin was in cahoots with Jackson and Nick. But Morgan couldn't be mad at her. Nick had sworn her to secrecy, and if there was one thing about Yavette, she didn't carry bones. Morgan snickered and decided to play along, but she couldn't wait to tell Nick.

"Umm, cuz. What part of this aren't you getting? I am not going on another blind date!" Morgan shouted into the phone, then looked up as Tina stepped into the office. *Oops, cat's out of the bag.*

"You don't have to get so testy. We'll talk about it again. But before you go, I need two favors."

Morgan rolled her eyes upward and released an exaggerated breath. "Sure, Yavette, what do you need?"

"You know Jackson and I are having a little get together for the wedding party next Saturday? I need you there. And I want to go shoe shopping. A new pair for the party would be nice."

"Okay, I'm up, for a little shoe shopping. Lets go to Sensual Steps. And yes, Yavette, I will be at the party. But, I gotta run, so I'll call you tomorrow." Morgan placed the phone back on its base. She looked up into the knowing eyes of Tina. She waved her hand. One day she'd tell it all, but today wasn't it. Rising from the desk, she gathered her personal items, tapped Tina on the shoulder, and left her office.

CHAPTER 14

At home, Morgan changed from her velour jogging suit to a wool, ankle length wrap skirt, a matching sweater and boots. She sprayed her twists with coconut oil, and refreshed her perfume and lipstick. When she heard the intercom, she glanced at her watch. It was seven on the head. She ran to the intercom, acknowledged her guest, then depressed the button that would gain him entry. Her foot tapped on the floor as she waited for his knock. Upon hearing it, she smoothed her hand down the front of her skirt, nodded her head absently, then opened the door. She smiled as the chocolate god, dressed to kill in a pair of dress olive slacks, a pale Lowden colored, collarless, pullover silk shirt and a mustard gold wool blazer. On his feet he wore a pair of professionally polished deep olive colored, cap toe shoes. He had a single red rose in his hand.

"Good evening, Morgan."

"Hi, Jarrod. Umm, I mean, Nick." She stepped to the side to allow him entry. "You know it's going to take me a minute to call you Nick." She shut the door behind him. He extended the rose to her. "Thank you."

"Not a problem."

They stood in the foyer, their eyes fastened on each other. Morgan fought the urge to step closer, erase the space between them, and wrap her arms around him while letting their lips mingle. She watched the slow, sexy smile spread across his face, causing her pulse to run away and beads of sweat began to form. Raising her bare hand, Morgan began to dab at the moisture forming on her upper lip.

"Here, let me take care of that," Nick said as he removed a hand-kerchief from the breast pocket of his mustard blazer. Gently, he dabbed at the moisture. He looked into her eyes, then down to her lips.

Morgan stood still as his face blurred and their lips met. Blindly, she reached out, placed the rose on the small table in the foyer, then brought her hands up and around Nick's back. She held on to him, her knees weakening under the sensuous fire caused by his hot kiss. Never, ever, had she felt a mind blowing kiss like the one she was experiencing. *Never.*

The sound of mews and whimpers interrupted them. Nick looked down at the cat rubbing its body along his lower legs, while the dog sat near his feet. He looked at Morgan and could see the heated passion in her eyes, the way her complexion had turned a deeper, reddening brown. He had started something he hoped he was up to finishing. He hadn't witnessed passion that deep and untapped before. "Who are these two?"

"Meet the Generals. Patton, the cat, and Davis, the dog." She pointed to one, then the other.

General Davis barked and Nick saluted the pets at his feet. "What interesting names."

"I got Patton first. When I got married, we lived in an apartment that had mice. I got Patton to chase the mice, and she is one hell of a mouser—was running the mice right out the door, like a general. After the divorce, Patton and I moved here. When I was moving in, I heard whining coming from a dumpster. I looked in and there he was, but he had the nerve to bark at me as I pulled him out of the dumpster. They run the place. I'm just here for their convenience."

Nick smiled. "I guess we should get going."

Morgan nodded, and grabbed her purse and keys. As she removed her coat from the hall tree, Nick took the article from her and held it for her to put on. His hands rested on her shoulders. She looked up into his eyes—hypnotic—and knew, in that moment, that she was falling hard for this brother, and she was powerless to do a thing about it but try to ride it out, not wishing or hoping past this day. She had loved only one man, Michael, and she wasn't sure if she could ever feel the same again. Yet Nick seemed so much more sure of himself, so secure.

They exited Morgan's condo. Nick took her hand in his as they entered the elevator. He pulled her closer to him and put his arm around her waist as he steered her out the building, down the block and around to corner to his vehicle. He opened the SUV's passenger door, waited until Morgan was in, shut the door and rounded the vehicle. Sliding behind the driver's seat, Nick started the car and headed to his house.

Once they arrived, Nick parked in the driveway and got out. He walked around to meet her. Taking his hand in hers, he led her to the front door, opened it, then stepped to the side to allow her entry.

"Nick, this is nice." She let him take her coat. "How long have you lived here?"

"About five years. I like living in the neighborhood. It's close to the bar and not far from downtown." He led her to the kitchen.

Her eyes widened. "Look at this kitchen." She turned and looked at him as he leaned his muscular frame against the door jam. "Can you really cook? Or are you perpetrating?"

Nick laughed aloud and headed to the refrigerator. He pulled out several meats. "Since you think I'm not the real McCoy, how about you go over there to that bathroom and wash your hands. You can help me perpetrate this fraud." He watched as she switched away to the bathroom off the kitchen.

Morgan returned to the sounds of smooth music. A glass of white wine sat on the butcher block. Nick was standing at the sink, his blazer gone. His wide back flexed as he rinsed off several pieces of fish. He turned and winked at her just before he gave orders on what to peel, slice and sauté. Forty minutes later, they sat down to Italian fare, beginning with a pasta and lentil soup, followed by stewed artichokes, salt cod with parsley and garlic as an entrée, and ending with tiramisu for desert.

"Okay, I was wrong," Morgan admitted. "You can get down. Who taught you how to cook?" She asked as he rose from the dinner table with plates in his hand. She picked up several from the table and followed him into the kitchen.

"My mother. She loved to cook and wasn't afraid to experiment, using us as guinea pigs, of course. She taught each of us how to cook and clean—to care for ourselves." She watched the forlorn expression shadow his eyes. "That's one of the many things I miss. My mom and I would swap new stuff to try, then laugh about how nasty it was if we made a mistake."

Morgan listened as he told her about his mother, her illness and death. "It's left a real void in this family."

"I bet."

"Tell me more about your family and Yavette." He loaded the dish washer, then put their deserts on a tray with two glasses. "Follow me." He said as they headed down a flight a stairs. He watched Morgan's expression. She seemed pleased. "Keep talking," he said as he pulled two DVDs from a shelf near the large plasma television. He placed them into the player. "Have a seat." He pointed to the theatre chairs, which were connected by a table, then walked over to the bar and grabbed two bottles of water from behind it.

Morgan looked around the large basement. The walls were paneled in a deep mahogany, a granite-top bar sat to one side, black high-back bar stools arranged neatly astride the bar, and a deep green, lit marble fireplace attached to the end. A recliner sat nearby. As she walked around, she told him about her large extended family, pausing ever so often to look at pictures and various posters arranged on the walls. She went on to tell how she and Yavette were related, and ended with her telling him that her father was a minister.

"A PC!"

"No, my dad didn't raise me like that. We didn't fall into the crazed trap folks try to set for children of ministers. If I didn't go to his church, I went to a church. We embrace all faiths. Dad's thing is, do you believe in a higher power. All else, he says, is pomp and circumstances." She thought about her father and looked at Nick. He had some of the same manners, holding doors, putting on a woman's coat. He even shared the same rich complexion as her dad. But she also knew that her dad would have a fit once he found out that Nick not only sold liquor, but owned the establishment as well. *Well, I'll cross that bridge if I come to it.* She ended by telling him of her conversation with Yavette.

"Okay," she continued, "then we'll let her keep thinking we don't know who the other is, then at the party we'll shock her somehow. Make sure when you talk to Jackson you don't tell him we're an item," she said as she settled back into the plush seats.

"I hope you don't mind, but I took the liberty of putting in a movie. It's one I think you'll like."

She watched as he picked up the remote. The screen flicked to life as the credits announced "Cabin in the Sky," the all-black musical released in 1943 staring Lena Horn, Ethel Waters and Louis Armstrong. Following that movie, they watched another race film, as they were called in the forties, called "Stormy Weather."

At the end of the second movie, Morgan stretched and looked at her watch. "Nick, do you know what time it is?"

"Time for us to go outside and play?" He lifted her hand and kissed the back of it.

She laughed. "No, crazy man. But it is getting late. I really should head home."

"I hear you. What are you doing tomorrow, outside of spending it with me?"

"Spending the day with you," she replied and looked at him.

"Then I guess I better get you home." He rose and put his hand out to her. She rose slowly from her sitting position and into his arms. He pulled her close and could feel the rapid beat of her heart. "I'm not going to hurt you, Morgan." He stared into her eyes. "And I'll never lie to you." His lips sealed his words as they claimed her, branded her all his—leaving no trace of doubt as to exactly what he meant. He felt her move and wanted to grab her hips and still them, least he lose control and take her right where they stood.

The moan started in the pit of her stomach, and no matter how hard she tried to stifle it, the sound rolled up and out. She felt him, the hardness of him as he pressed her closer. Her hands took on their own mind as she began to caress his back, rubbing her hands up and down, then up to capture his smooth face in her hands. The throbbing in her feminine core startled her—made her aware of the fact that she hadn't been intimate since her divorce nearly three years ago. If he didn't stop with the sweet torture, the nips to her lips, the playful, yet sensuous way he pulled on her tongue then intimated the most intimate act, she would strip him bare!

"Umm, Nick."

"Hmmm," came his response as he continued the lip-searing assault.

"If we don't stop now, we'll never stop." She placed her hands on his biceps and felt them flex through his denim shirt. She wanted to feel him—all of him minus the clothing. She wanted to see him, the dark chocolate over his muscular frame. She felt his lips upon hers again, this time forcing her mouth open and purposely, languidly played, nipped, teased and suckled. Her knees buckled as he lightly sucked on her bottom lip, pulling it in, then releasing it right before he kissed her, then placed his tongue in her mouth. This was unreal! She had never met a man who was such an expert at kissing, much less seemed to derive great pleasure from such a simple, yet sensuous act.

They, this, seemed so right—as if they were meant to be here and nowhere else. A slight whimper escaped her throat when he pulled back. "Don't make me stop, baby. Tell me I can have you."

She looked into his darkening eyes. Fear and game was not what she saw. She saw a heightened passion and a need so great she began to ache. She nodded her head and felt him take her into his arms. She wrapped her arms around his neck as he picked her up and walked over to the recliner. He sat down and began to nibble at her neck. She moaned loudly.

"You smell so good, woman. I just want to feel you," he said through clinched teeth. His hands trailed slowly up her back as his mouth claimed hers once again, feasting on the carnage he was leaving behind with every kiss. She was coming undone. If he didn't quit soon, she knew she would lose what little control she had been holding on to.

"And you feel good, too." He placed his hand under her sweater and softly massaged her back, running his hand up under her bra strap. As she sat on his lap, she felt the beginning of his hardened state. She was close, but not close enough to feel him entirely. He pulled her sweater upward and unsnapped her bra with one hand. Goose bumps raised all along her body as his hand wrapped around her and slowly eased up to her breast. His mouth trailed down her neck. She watched as his head disappeared under her sweater. She held her breath as she waited. If his mouth on her breast felt anything like it did on her mouth, she was in trouble. Or more like he was in trouble.

"Stop me now, woman, if this isn't what you want." He breathed, then slowly pulled her nipples into his hot mouth. Her hips gyrated backward as his free hand tried to still her, to reign in the passion that was about to erupt between them both. The more he sucked, the more she gyrated, until finally, they both had enough. He rose with her in his arms and placed her on the recliner. He knelt before her, removed her sweater and red lace bra. He held the bra in his hands and shook his head. However, there was no stopping now—the only way to put out this fire was to have her and no other would do.

"Can I undress you, Morgan?"

What was she going to say? No? She was partially undressed, her bare breasts illuminated by the flames dancing in the fireplace. She nodded her head, then stood and watched as he unbuttoned her skirt, letting it fall to the floor before him. He rubbed his hands up her tights-clad legs until he reached the band. He slipped his fingers in them and eased them down, taking her boots off with them. Sitting back on his haunches, his eyes drank her in, standing before him dressed in nothing but a pair of red lace panties. He inhaled deeply, returned to his kneeling position, hooked his thumbs into the waist of her panties, and tugged them slowly down her body.

"Umph." He sucked in air and shook his head as he eyed her from the tips of her painted toenails, to the v of her femininity, up her full breasts with the large nipple, to her beautiful face. He rose to stand over her and pulled his shirt over his head, letting the garment fall to floor next to hers. He watched her eyes dart around the room. He gently pulled her face to his. "No, don't look away. I want you to see me." He continued to undress until finally he was naked. He pulled her to him. She felt the hard length of him and sighed. He rubbed his body against hers, causing her hips to jut forward. She wanted him and knew that the moment they joined she would forever be his—no questions asked.

"No, not yet. I want you wet and ready for me, woman." He motioned for her to sit back on the recliner. He descended to his knees and began kissing her feet, then rubbed them across his chest. She giggled at the feel of his hairy chest on her feet. He smiled up at her, then winked at her. His hands rubbed her calves as he kissed her knees, then her thighs. He pulled her closer to the edge and kissed her everywhere but there. Her mind raced. His mouth was assaulting her senses, making her moan and squirm. And though the assault was wonderful, she wanted to feel him inside of her.

He sat back and pulled her hips, his nose inches from her folds. She felt him kiss her, gently, then felt his tongue ply apart the folds to find the hidden jewel. She bucked forward, and he held her hips in his large hands as he feasted upon her, his tongue doing its own wicked dance, edging her toward an explosion. Her hips began to move slowly, and then increased as he increased the pressure.

Morgan grabbed his head and screamed as an orgasm tore through her body, leaving her spent. He continued to feast, like a man hungry for more, and she allowed him to until she could stand it no more. She pulled his head upward and looked at him as she joined him on the floor. Rising above him, she eased her body onto his, and teased him, slowly going down so far then pulling up, her muscles tightened as she did. She watched his eyes turn a dangerous dark as he grabbed her hips.

"Hold on, baby. I want to marry you, but do we want children right now?" He held her hips as he came to a sitting position, the core of her dangerously close. "Please go into the bathroom over there to the left and look in the medicine cabinet. There's some condoms there." Morgan cocked her head to the right. "Any excuse to watch you walk."

She smiled at his admission, rose and went to the bathroom. She returned and stood over him, taking in the smooth, cut lines of his muscles. She held out the condom. He took it as his face buried itself once more into her folds. Her head tossed back as the assault began again, making her knees shake and her body quiver. He eased back and pulled Morgan to ease onto him. She gasped as she felt the large hardness slip inside of her—the fit of him. They held on as he sunk further inside of her. Together they moved, rocked, and twisted as they gave of themselves unselfishly.

Nick knew that this was far from over. He was just beginning to show this woman how much he cared about her. To him this was just the icing on the cake, the ultimate act of emotions. His heart constricted as he felt drops of water on his chest. He looked up to see the tears drop from her eyes onto his chest. He held her close to his chest and moved with her as her emotions overcame her.

"This is real, baby," he said. "Don't fear it, don't fear me. This is real." They moved faster, the feelings mixed with the passion was at eruption—was about to blow.

Morgan threw her head back. Her toes curled, and she moaned loudly as the wicked sensation took over and tossed her afloat. Moments later, she felt him throb as he pushed in and out of her, his hands tightly around her, holding her close to his chest as if she would float away. His seed spilled into the condom. He groaned as her muscles contracted around him, and he became rigid again.

He rolled her over and began again. Her hips thrust upward to meet his. Her arms wrapped around his back as they held on to each other and let the passion sweep them up, hold them, then hurl them forward to a never ending vortex. As she cried out his name, he pumped into her furiously. Her legs wrapped around his waist. *This cannot be,* he thought as the warm sensation overwrought his entire body and left him spent as he achieved yet another release.

Carefully, Nick eased himself from her, discarded the condom, then pulled a throw from atop a nearby theatre seat and wrapped it around them as Morgan came to lie atop his body. He held her in his arms. Her head nestled under his chin. She listened to his heart as the beats began to return to normal. She smiled when she thought about what her cousins had said about getting your toes curled. The brother had definitely curled her toes.

She rested on his broad chest, inhaling the masculine scent of him mixed with cologne. Her eyes drifted close as she snuggled closer to him. Her hands held his arms tightly.

"Are you okay, Morgan?"

She nodded her head and tried to snuggle into him closer. She thought about his words and the fact that they had made love. Could it be true? Did she hear him when he said he wanted to marry her? *Wow*. And at thirty-two she had just got her toes curled for the first time. Later she thought she heard voices, then felt a large blanket cover her as her body was lifted and carried away. She was too satiated to wake, for her body had gone into a peaceful slumber she didn't want to wake from. Tomorrow—she'll ask tomorrow.

CHAPTER 15

Saturday morning she stretched, her arm hit something solid. She rolled over and looked up into the eyes of Nick smiling down at her.

"Good morning. I trust you slept well."

"I did. What did you do, spike my water?" She laughed and rolled over to face him. She noted that she was naked under the covers.

"No such thing, but Nehemiah came home and found us on the floor."

"Aww, no!"

"Don't worry, only David was with him. I didn't show him much, just a leg, with plenty of thigh," he said. Morgan watched as his face was serious, but his eyes held mischief.

"Mr. Chambers, you better be joking."

"Only about the David part and showing your legs. But Nehemiah did see us wrapped up."

Morgan hid her face in her hands. "What did you do?"

"He tossed me a blanket. I covered us up and carried you up here. And you've been asleep ever since."

"What time is it?"

"Five."

"In the morning?" She watched as he nodded his head yes.

"What are you doing today?"

"I have to head into the office. I may have an overnight trip next Friday, but I'll be back in time for the party. I need to get ready for my trip. What about you?"

"Nothing." He moved closer to her and put his arm on her waist. She scooted over and closed the space, feeling the hard, muscular length of him. Admittedly, she loved his body and they way he made hers sizzle. He leaned his head down and began to nibble on her neck.

She raised her head to give him better access just as he began to worry her nipple with the pads of his fingers.

Rolling over atop her, he rested his weight on his elbows as he watched her. Wrapping her arms around his neck, she kissed him, then stroked the stubble on his cheek and outlined his thick mustache with the tip of her fingers. Bracing himself with one hand, his free hand reached out to caress her side, stopping at the tip of her nipple. He lowered his head and captured a nipple between his teeth.

"Nick," she moaned out his name, which became the undoing as he reached out to the nightstand, grabbed a condom, tore the package, rolled it over his hard penis, and grabbed her by the hips.

As they moved, they knew this was just the beginning.

For the rest of the week, Morgan and Nick spent every day with each other, after work, during work, when he'd come by bearing lunch. They were basking in the simple fact that they were falling in love—and for once, they mused, neither was afraid of tomorrow. The only thing that remained unresolved was when she would tell her father all about Nick. Skip Yavette, who had called several times to remind her about their shoe shopping on Friday—she was the least of Morgan's problems. But she knew one thing for sure, and that was she'd fallen hard for Nicholas Jarrod Chambers, Jr., and there wasn't a damn thing anyone could say or do to change that, not even her father.

Early Thursday morning, Morgan's phone rang. She reached over Nick's large back and grabbed it.

"Hello," she spoke into the phone as her head hid in Nick's back. She stifled a giggle as he rolled over and began to awaken her body.

"Hey, Morgan, how are you, gorgeous?"

"Who's this?" She couldn't imagine who would be calling her this time of the morning outside of family.

"Tony. I meant to call you and apologize about that night, but I've had so much happen to me, you wouldn't believe it." Morgan looked up to see Nick leaning over her. She was sure he could hear Tony on the line. He held his hand out for the phone. She handed it to him and watched as he hung up on Tony.

"You snooze, you lose," he said, then pulled her on top of him. She felt the heat of his erection and began moving against him just as the phone rang again. Looking at Nick, she raised her eyebrows. He nodded his head and answered the phone.

"How can I help you?" He listened to the response before speaking. "Dude, this is Morgan's boyfriend. And I want to thank you for standing her up, because had you not, I wouldn't be here. So, take the hint, and don't call here anymore. Later." He hung up the phone and continued teasing Morgan into a frenzy.

Just as they satisfied their need of each other, the phone rang again. Morgan nodded for him to answer it.

"Hello. Morgan's man here," he said, then sat up straight. Morgan watched his face as it contorted. He handed her the phone.

"Hello," she spoke into the phone, then sat straight up in bed as her face blanched. It was her father, Reverend Ishmael Paige, the no-nonsense man who believed in honesty and integrity and had always insisted that his "baby girl" do as such.

"Would you like to tell me why a man is answering your phone at six in the morning?"

Morgan sighed and raked her fingers through her twists. She wanted to sit down and talk to him about Nick, not discuss him over the phone. She watched as Nick rose from the bed and tipped to the bathroom as if her father could hear him—the floor was covered by carpet.

"Dad, you always insisted I speak truth. Well, that was Nicholas, he's my boyfriend, and he spent the night here." She listened at the silence, which was awkward, seeing as how they had rarely disagreed about anything. She could not really recall a time she and her father ever argued—no one in the family was the arguing type.

At sixty-six, Ishmael Paige had worked for almost his entire life at the steel mill while preaching on the weekends at various churches. He had started preaching when he was eighteen, not long after he began working at the steel mills in Indiana. Her mother, Norma, the same age as her father, had been the head nurse for one of the county's long-term care facilities. They had both retired at the same time and now seemed to be enjoying a life of pure leisure. Morgan snickered at the memory of walking in on her parents as they lounged lazily on the couch, draped in each others' arms and very much naked. She wondered why he was up so early.

"I know that's not what you wanted to hear, Dad, but I'm very much grown. I'd like for you and Nick to meet."

"What does he do for a living?"

Oh, oh! How in God's name am I going to get past this? She knew her dad would have a fit if not give birth to a calf. "I'll tell you, but please put mom on the extension." She waited as she heard her father tell her mother that she was wanted on the phone and to pick up the extension. Morgan looked up and saw Nick standing in doorway to her bathroom, a white towel wrapped low about his waist. She shook her head, thinking now was not the time for erotic thoughts, but he did look scrumptious standing there. She waved him over to sit next to her on the bed.

"Okay, your mother's on the other the line. So what does the young man do for a living, Morgan?"

She swallowed hard and held Nick's hand. "He's a business owner."

"Baby, what type of businesses?" her mother asked.

"Well, Nick owns a few investment properties. He's a partial owner in a spa/resort up in Lake Geneva and a place called Nick's."

"Nick's," Her father repeated. "Wait. Is it that place on 71st? The sports bar? Morgan!" Her father's voice boomed though the phone. She held if from her ear as he went into a tirade over the wages of sin being in the bottom of a liquor bottle.

"Mom!" Morgan called into the phone.

"And I'll not have my daughter, my only child, traipsing around with a man who sells the devil's brew. I'll not have it!"

"Dad, you are tripping. Folks who drink do so because they want to, not forced to. And it's only a sin if you fall into a drunken state," she said.

Wait a minute, she thought, *I'm a grown ass woman and have been for a long time. There's no way I'm going to sit here and defend Nick to a man who never forgave his father.* "You know what your problem is, Dad? You haven't forgiven Grandpa Mack," she accused him, then heard her mother gasp. "You may want to think you have, but you haven't. I'm crazy about Nick, and I want to be with him. Dad, you'd like Nick. He reminds me of you." She heard the line click.

"Baby, your father hung up," her mother spoke into the phone.

"That's fine. Are you going to stand with him?"

"He's my husband, Morgan. Yes, you are my child, and I love you, and will honor you as my adult child, but when you marry again, maybe you will realize that you must stand by your mate, disagree between the two of you and not in front of people." Morgan inhaled deeply, then heard her mother say in a whisper, "You and Nick meet me for lunch at 12:30." Morgan smiled. "Goodbye, dear."

"Bye, Mom." Morgan placed the phone on its base and looked at Nick. She looked down at his hand. She'd held his hand so tightly that her nails made indentations in the palm of his hand. She kissed his palm. "Sorry. So, I guess you know."

He pulled her onto his lap. "Doesn't frighten me. He'll come around. And my dad wants to meet you. He wants us to come by after your flight lands Saturday. We'll meet up with him, and then head to the party."

She kissed him on the cheek and hugged him. She didn't want to leave him, but she had to attend the Espy Awards Friday night in LA where Willie and Keith were both nominated in several categories. But she knew that once the affair was over, she'd be on a red eye back home to Nick.

Looking at his face, she thought that nothing seemed to rattle him. His even temperament was the respite she wanted after fighting with her father for the first time in years. The thought of never speaking to her father again saddened her. The only other time she had disobeyed her father was when she chose to get married in Jamaica, versus the church he headed. Outside of that, they had always been close. She went, like her mother, along with Rev. Paige because he had always been a fair and honest person. Morgan wished he could just move on, but he seemed stuck on this one issue. One that would stand between them.

"Come, let's get dressed. I've got a business meeting about that property in Indiana, and you need to go to work." He picked her up, kissed her on the forehead and walked with her in his arms to the bathroom, making love slow and easy in the shower as she felt the love of him roll over her like the water beading down their bodies. It was the balm she'd needed.

Morgan walked into her office and instantly noticed the bouquet of red roses sitting on Tina's desk. She stopped at the desk and smiled at her assistant. "Come on in the office. I've got something to tell you." They entered Morgan's office. She sat at her the table and watched as Tina sat across from her. "Where should I begin?" Morgan sat back and told Tina about her ill-fated dates. When she was done, Tina had jumped up from her desk and hugged her boss.

"I knew you were more than the surface. I always wondered when you'd let the real Morgan out. Finally, you went on an adventure, and look what you've got. Nehemiah's fine brother." Tina hugged her again. "And I wasn't sure if I should tell you or not, but I was there with Nehemiah the same night you spent with Nick."

"Oh my goodness. Please tell me you didn't see us." Morgan looked at Tina, sure a look of horror was plastered on her face.

"I didn't' see anything." She winked. "Other than Nick carrying you up the stairs in his arms. I was envious, because we were in the basement." Tina chuckled.

They laughed and discussed the Chambers brothers, agreeing that they were one-of-a-kind men and that their mother most definitely had raised good men and not coddled little boys posing as men. At a quarter to noon, she looked up to see Nehemiah, followed by Nick, standing in the doorway to her office. Nick had been there, but this was Nehemiah's first time. She had Tina give him the tour as Nick sat on the leather couch on the other side of the office.

"Close the door, baby."

Morgan laughed and shook her head no. She knew that if she did, he and her would be naked in no time, and her mother was due to arrive at any moment. "No way, Mr. Chambers. We'll be doing something we shouldn't."

He rose, closed and locked the door, and then walked over to her. Morgan could see that the gold flecks in his light eyes had turned a burnt copper as he got closer to her. She backed up to the desk as he pulled her to him. He looked at his watch. "What time is your mom coming by?" He kissed her on the side of her neck, nipping at that section right above her collar bone. She shivered.

"Umm, baby, you smell good, and I like this blouse. Can I see what's under it?" He kissed her again, and she shuddered. "What's wrong, baby? Are you going to answer my questions?" He chuckled as he took her face in his hands and traced her lips with his thumbs. "Have I told you that you are one irresistible woman?" He leaned forward and kissed her lips as he pulled her skirt up.

"Umm, you must have known," he said as he noticed the garter holding up thigh high stockings and the flimsy strip of a pair of panties. He played in her pubic hair as his fingers sought and found the jewel hidden in her folds. She arched her back, thrusting her hips forward as he circled the jewel, bringing her to a vicious climax. As she came down, he placed her legs around his waist. He kept kissing her, attacking her with the soft, yet insistent onslaught of his sensuous kisses.

Nick groaned aloud when he felt her hand touch him just as she pulled his zipper down and freed him from his pants. In one fluid thrust, they were joined, their bodies moving as he unbuttoned her blouse and pulled her bra above her breasts. He lowered his head and took turns laving each nipple until he heard her call out his name. Thrusting languidly in and out her tight, warm body, he knew that he was close to feeling that release only her body could ignite. He lost it as she tightened her core around his thick flesh and grabbed his head as she came hard, followed by him. They continued to move against each other as the aftershocks ripped through their bodies, bathing them in a lover's sheen. Morgan looked up at him and realized that they hadn't used protection. She hid her head in his chest.

"What's the matter, baby?"

"We didn't use protection. And I'm ovulating." She watched his face to gage his reaction to what she had just said to him. If he knew human anatomy, then he should know what she meant. When his expression didn't change, she wondered why. "Do you know what it means, Nick?"

He kissed her on the lips. "Sure do. It means that in three to five days you could be carrying my son or daughter. Then we would get married sooner, rather than later. I don't want your father to shoot me on top of not liking me." He kissed her again and looked at his watch. "Your mom will be here in fifteen minutes." They quickly dressed.

Fifteen minutes later, Norma Paige walked into Morgan's office. She hugged Morgan tightly to her, and then stood back and looked up at Nick as he stood next to Morgan. He put his hand out to her.

"Mrs. Paige, it's a pleasure meeting you."

"Same here, Nick." She sat at the table in Morgan's office. "So, what are your plans for my daughter?" The words came out without hesitation. Nick nodded her head and sat next to her.

"Let me assure you, Mrs. Paige, my intentions are purely selfish." He flashed her mother a megawatt smile, dimples and all. "I want to date and eventually marry your daughter. I know that Rev. Paige isn't too sweet on my owning a bar that serves liquor, but know that no one in my family has more than one drink on any given day."

Morgan left her mother and Nick to order sandwiches from the corner deli. After the sandwiches arrived, Tina and Nehemiah sat down with Morgan, Nick and Mrs. Paige. After two hours of laughter and discussions of everything under the sun, including marriage and children, Morgan's mom stood and embraced Nick.

"I'll have a chat with Reverend Paige. Maybe he'll change his mind."

Morgan walked out with her mother. They embraced.

"Child, I know what you mean. He's a lot like your father: protective, fearless and secure. No wonder you're crazy about him. And he is quite handsome."

"Thank you, Mom. So, you'll talk to Dad?"

"I'll will, baby. I will talk to him and let you know. I can't make any promises, but I will talk to him."

After her mother left, followed by Nick and Nehemiah, and they cleaned up the refuse from the sandwiches, it was half past four in the afternoon. Morgan had promised Yavette they would meet at Sensuous Steps.

She grabbed her purse and coat and rushed out the door to meet Yavette.

Once the cab rolled to a stop, Morgan jumped out and rushed up to the door. Thank God, she knew the owner, because Sensuous Steps closed at five and it was fifteen after. She smiled at Nicole James, the owner, as she opened the door. They embraced warmly.

"Looking good, sister," Morgan said as she looked her friend up and down. "Where's Yavette?"

"Girl, she's in the back picking out more shoes than she can even carry. She told me that she's getting married, so she's trying to pick out bridesmaid's shoes." Nicole stepped closer. "I think you better go get her, she done picked out three pairs of stilettos." They laughed as Morgan and Nicole walked hand in hand toward the back. Morgan laughed aloud as she watched her cousin surrounded by several pairs of shoes. Yavette looked up and held a pair of hot pink stilettos.

"Aren't these cute?"

"Umm, sure, girl. But they are CFM shoes," Morgan replied. "They say: if you are looking to have your brains screwed out, do wear me." They laughed as Morgan took the shoes from Yavette's hands and placed them on the shelf. She looked around the store, the bright, exposed brick, adorned with pink wall hangings and over stuffed beige chairs. Morgan saw a pair of mustard colored, high-heeled boots. She slipped her shoes off and tapped them lightly on the coolness of the highly glossed hard wood floors. Nicole brought her the boots to try on. Instantly, Morgan loved them and placed them in a pile to purchase.

For over an hour, Yavette, Nicole and Morgan laughed and talked, while Morgan and Yavette picked out several pairs of shoes and another pair of boots. As they tallied up the numbers of shoes, Morgan stepped over to the rear rack. She picked up a pair of shoes, turning to show them to Yavette.

"What are your colors?"

"Black and white."

Morgan brought the shoes back to Yavette. "Look at these. These are cute." She held up the suede shoes with the 2-inch heel, a feather situated on the front. "Nicole, I think these are the shoes for the wedding. What do you think, Yavette?"

She took the shoe from Morgan and felt the sole, rubbing her hand along the body of the shoe. "This is really nice. Nicole, can you order six pairs of these on short notice? The wedding is in six months, and I need to get you the shoe sizes."

"Six months?" Morgan looked at Yavette, her mouth wide open.

"Yeah, Jackson and I are getting married in April."

"When were you going to tell me?" Morgan said and looked from Nicole and back to Yavette. "There's a lot of planning that needs to take place."

"I know, Morgan, but we can pull it off. I know we can."

Morgan felt her cell phone vibrate in the bottom of her bag. She fished it out and looked at the caller-ID. She rose from the chair and walked to the front of the store. Her smiled widened.

"Hey, baby, where are you?"

"Spending a short fortune on shoes and a pair of boots."

"What color are the boots?"

"Gold, and they are too cute."

"Will you model only them for me?"

"Ahh, you're bad. But I'll wear them for you, sweetheart."

"I can't wait. What time are you heading my way?"

"I should see you in about an hour. Where do you want me to come to?"

"Come to the bar. I'll take you home to pack, and then I'll drop you off at the office in the morning. We'll meet up with my dad before I take you to the airport."

"Okay, baby. I'll see you later."

He rang off. Morgan placed the phone back in her purse, turned and came face to face with Yavette. She noticed her eyes were narrowed.

"Who were you talking to? Calling them baby?"

"A friend. No one you know." She dismissed Yavette with a wave of her hand, waltzed past her, then headed to the counter to purchase the three pairs of shoes and the pair of boots she had selected. Yavette joined her. She could see Yavette was eyeing her. Morgan steeled herself. Let her sweat it, but wait until she saw who the "baby" was.

Two hours later, she was at home packing for her overnight trip to LA. Once finished, she left with Nick and spent the night lying in his arms, basking in the glow of how he was making her feel—loved, cherished and protected.

As she drifted off to sleep, she held onto him, wrapped her arms about him and knew at that moment she loved him. And though she thought she had loved Michael, something in her feelings for Nick was different. She wanted to be with him as much as possible, and when they loved, her entire soul sang. Her falling in love with him had changed her. For once in her life, Morgan had felt at peace with a man.

She had not wondered or worried about Nick, how he felt about her. He never let the hour go by without either telling her or showing her. And odd enough, a part of her wanted to bear children, and if she had gotten pregnant, so be it. She'd be giving birth to a Chambers and would marry Nick without further conversation. *That's love,* she thought. *Real love.*

CHAPTER 16

Nick watched Morgan walk into the bar from the one-way mirror on the door to his office, which allowed him to see out, but blocked anyone from seeing inside. He noticed that she had pulled her twists back from her round face. He liked it. To him, it gave her face an angelic bent to it. He made a mental note to tell her how much he liked it. Heck, he wanted to tell her that he had fallen in love with her. He didn't' realize it until after he had made love to her that morning in the shower, and she had held on to him. At that moment, he didn't want to let her go—wanted to protect her from the seen and the unseen. He did not want to spend his life without her in it. Somehow she had seeped into his mind, body and soul, and he had no intentions of ever letting her go.

He looked at his watch. He needed to get her to the airport for her flight to California. He placed his hand on the doorknob, then stopped short when he saw a man approach her, say something to her, then take her hand in his and lead her to a seat at the bar.

As he observed the scene, the hairs on his body rose quickly and his eyes narrowed as he watched the man's mouth move rapidly. He had just seen this dude some twenty minutes earlier as he waltzed in, looking around the bar as if he didn't approve of what he was seeing before him, then grab another woman by the hand and engage her in conversation right before writing something on a napkin and handing it over.

Nick cursed under his breath. He had never seen Morgan with a man, and he didn't like the inexplicable, sudden surge of jealousy that washed over him. He continued to watch them as Morgan gave him a slight smile. He twisted his lips at the scene as the man stopped the flower vendor in the bar, purchased a single red rose and handed it to Morgan.

"Aww, hell naw," he spat out and stopped just as his father came to stand by his side.

"Boy, who you cursing at?

"Nothing." He turned to embrace his father. "How are you doing?"

"Good. Bones are acting right today. Where's this Miss Morgan at?"

"She just walked in. We've got about a half an hour before I need to get her to the airport for her flight."

"Is that her talking to the guy?

Nick nodded his head.

"She's pretty. You done good. David and Nehemiah have been talking about her." He stood at the mirror and watched her. "Wait," Nick Sr. began. "She looks familiar." He took his glasses from his pants pockets, wiped the lenses on his shirt, then placed them on his face. "That's Morgan Paige."

"How do you know her?" Nick asked.

"I don't. Not personally. I read an article on her some time ago in Chicago Woman. She owns her own company. Girl gots spunk. Represents several pro athletes, including William 'Willie' Johnson, the wide receiver for Tennessee."

Nick smiled proudly at the facts.

"And this is where y'all met?" Nick Sr. asked. Nick watched as his father got that infamous gleam in his eyes just as he began his trip down memory lane. His father said he had opened the bar six months before he met Lorene. According to his father, he was in love the moment she stepped inside the bar. They dated for one year before marrying. To Nick Sr., the opening of the bar and his meeting the woman he married, and who bore him three healthy sons, was a blessing to him, but after her death, two years ago, he'd lost interest in the upkeep and day-to-day operation.

Nick Sr. looked back out of the window. "And you met her here?" he asked again.

Nick nodded in response.

"Well, you better get out there and claim your woman, son." He chuckled and pointed to the man sitting close to Morgan. "Hey, he looks familiar."

"You know him?"

"If I'm not wrong, his father used to be a regular in here. A real jack-of-all trades. Never quite knew what that man did. But he always had a hustle." Nick Sr. continued to stare out of the mirror. "Yeah, that's Bill Martin's boy, Tony." He looked at his son. "And that boy is just like him. Always got some sort of hustle. You know, I believe that boy got into some trouble a while back. Caught a case. Had to do some time in a fed walk-around."

"Prison, Dad?" Nick raised his eyebrow.

"Yeah." Nick Sr. nodded. "He's a thief. Well, at least that's what folks say he went to jail for. Embezzlement and fraud. This was a couple of years back. Seems as if Tony there had a thing for older women. Would gain their trust, and then rob them blind. Suppose to have used their credit cards and withdrew money from their accounts without them knowing it."

It was time for them to head out. He would suggest his father ride with them to the airport, that way he'd get a chance to really talk to Morgan. "Pops, how about you ride to the airport with us?" He grabbed his coat and opened the door. He hadn't heard his father, or seen anything other than red, as he neared Morgan and overheard the man talking to her.

"Hey, I said I was sorry, and I even bought you a rose. What's your problem?"

"Tony, I told you, I'm not interested. Now if you don't mind, I need to go." She rose, and the man grabbed her by the wrist. Nick rushed forward, whipped Morgan behind him, grabbed Tony by his collar and snatched him close.

"You ever lay a hand on my woman again, you can forget walking, much less crawling." Nick pushed him out of the door and watched as he hit the concrete pavement. Nick put his hand out to Morgan, then stepped past the man sprawled out on the concrete. Craig laughed as they passed.

Nick reached his SUV and opened both passenger doors, then rounded the vehicle. Morgan looked back to see a man coming up the rear. Instantly, she knew it was Nick's father. She waited until he reached the vehicle.

Morgan extended her hand and found herself in a bear hug.

"No need for formalities, you're going to be my daughter one of these days soon." He pulled back and winked at her. "Name's Nick Sr., but folks outside of my boys call me Big Nicky. And if my boy wasn't so smitten with ya, I'd take you out myself." He hugged her again, then motioned for her to get in the SUV. He closed the door, and then climbed behind her.

She stole a glance at Nick, his eyes narrowed and his jaw taut. He flexed, as if he'd been slapped, when she reached out and touched his hand.

"What's the matter, Nick?"

"Who was that guy all over you?" he looked over at her. She could see by the change in color of his eyes that he was truly angry. But she had no idea that Tony would be in the bar, much less knew how she looked. She then remembered that Yavette had shown him a picture of her.

"Baby, that was the same guy you hung up on the other day. I had no idea he was coming to the bar."

He looked over at her. She noticed his features soften as she rubbed his forearm.

"Sorry, I hope he's okay."

As he drove to the airport, Nick's father and Morgan talked. She laughed as he told story after story about Nick and his brothers growing up, and the days when he ran the bar with the help of Mr. Johnson.

As they reached the departure area outside of O'Hare Airport, Nick and his father climbed out of the vehicle. Nick, Sr., reached for Morgan's hand as Nick Jr. grabbed her overnight case. Nick, Sr., hugged her again, kissed her on the cheek and wished her a safe flight.

She and Nick walked to the curbside check in. He pulled her into his arms and nestled his nose in the top of her twists before he leaned down and kissed her on the lips. "Will that hold you until you return?"

Smiling, she nodded her head and kissed him again. "No more fighting, Mr. Chambers."

"No more blind dates," he said as he winked his eye at her. He pulled her back into his arms, kissed her again and told her to call him once she landed.

Promising to contact him, she watched him as he walked back to his vehicle, slapping his father on the shoulder as he rounded. He paused at the door, waved, then got in and drove off,

"Flight 321 to Los Angeles now boarding at gate E17. All passengers for flight 321 please head to gate E17," cracked the voice overhead. Morgan hurried down the long corridor, stopped at the check-in counter, handed over her ticket, completed the usual ritual, then was allowed to board the plane. She settled in her seat, pulled her headphones and the latest Tamara Hale mystery from her briefcase, then buckled her seatbelt. The four-hour flight would give her time to do a little reading, as well as a little work. In addition, the time would give her time to sort out her feelings about Nick. She knew she loved him, but she also wanted to be sure that he felt the same. She thought about her father and hoped her mother had spoken to him, told him what a wonderful man Nick was.

As the plane descended, Morgan closed her eyes briefly, saying a silent prayer. When she opened them, she was met by the billowy clouds passing out her window seat in first class. She wondered what Nick was doing.

Later, when she touched down in Los Angeles, she knew that her life had changed, and she had to tell him that she had fallen in love with him. But, she also knew that a part of her had fallen for him the moment she met him. This was just the icing on the cake, so to speak. Once she returned, she knew she had to tell him. Had to tell him that she had fallen in love with him.

After working most of the evening and late into the night at the bar, Nick had spoken with Nehemiah about Morgan. He knew he loved her, and there was no way around it—not that he wanted to. But he had his heart broken once, real good, and he wanted to make sure. Yet, each time he looked into Morgan's eyes, he saw the love in them whether she told him or not.

He needed to speak to his father. He knew that his father didn't go to bed early, and after he closed at two on the dot, he drove over to his father's house.

He let himself in the house with the key he always kept on his ring. As he entered the living room, soft light from the small lamp set upon a mahogany end table allowed him to see the various pictures of him and his family on the cream-colored walls. One picture in particular caused him to pause. The picture of his mother and father smiled down on him. His mother's warm glow reminded him of Morgan. He stared at his mother's face, then looked away and continued toward his father's room.

"Nicky, that you, boy?"

"Yeah, Dad. It's me." Nick appeared in the doorway of his father's new room. New, because his father had moved into the room Nick had shared with David. His father no longer wanted to sleep in the room he had shared with his wife of over forty years.

"What's wrong? Morgan land safely?"

"Yeah, she called me." He looked at his watch. "She should be just leaving the awards."

"So, what's on your mind?"

Nick laughed at how transparent he was around his parents. "Remember you said you'd know when the person was right, that you wouldn't be able to get them out of your system?"

"I remember. I felt that way about your mother. Do you feel that way about Morgan?"

Nick sat down on the recliner next to his father's bed. He looked at the man who taught him what it meant to be a real man: honesty, keeping your word, work for what you got, and take care of the ones you love. "Yes, I do, Dad. But her father is a minister and dead set against her going out with me, so I know he won't give us his blessing."

"Son, we can't deal with his hypocrisy. You love Morgan, and I think she'll make you a great wife. So, deal straight from the top. Y'all grown. She doesn't need anyone's approval. Yeah, we want our parents to like our mates, but do we really care? Hell naw. I know I didn't. Lorene's mother couldn't stand me, but I married her daughter anyway, and told her that she could either get with it or move on. After a while she came to like me, but it wasn't anything I did. I didn't feel I had to please but one person. Your momma."

"I hear you. I just don't want her to look at me later and blame me for the rift. I'm willing to sell the bar to Nehemiah or David if it'll make the difference."

"Boy, don't be crazy. She'll be angry at herself if she thought that she forced you into that. Don't worry about him. What did you say his name was?"

"I didn't, but his name is Ishmael Paige."

Nick Sr. nodded his head. "Are you going to ask Morgan to marry you?"

"Yes."

"Good," he said as he rose from the bed. "I've got something for you." Nick watched as his father left the room, and returned moments later with a black box. He sat on the edge of the bed and opened the box. He held up a strand of pearls. "These belonged to your mother. David got the engagement ring cause he was the first to marry. You get the necklace to give to Morgan." He handed Nick the precious pearls and left the room to return the case to its hiding place. He returned and climbed back into bed. "You spending the night?"

"Sure, why not?" Nick replied as his father tossed him a pillow and the blanket at the foot of the bed. He reclined the chair and continued to talk to his father until they both dozed off. As sleep claimed Nick, he thought of Morgan lying in his arms, and though they had officially been dating a week, he knew that he had strong feelings for her. There was no way he could go back to being without her.

Morgan stepped through the crowd that had gathered near the entrance. Her eyes searched out and found the one person she knew would be there. She smiled as she walked toward him. His light eyes rested upon her. She rushed toward him as he opened his arms to her. The smiling dimples propelled her forward. He pulled her to him as she reached where he stood.

"You're here. Thank you."

"Morgan, I'm going to always be here. But I need to know two things." He released her and looked down at her. "One, are the blind dates really over?"

"Yes, Nick. I don't want to be with anyone but you. And what's the second thing?" she asked and watched as he got down on one knee and took her hand in his. People walking around them went *ooh* and *ahh* with several stopping to watch as Nick looked up into Morgan's eyes.

"Morgan, I love you, and I want you to marry me. I know it's sudden. We can have a long engagement if you like, but I want to know that this ring says you are mine and I'm yours?" He pulled a diamond solitaire from his coat pocket and placed the ring on the ring finger of her left hand.

Tears streamed down her cheek as she nodded her head up and down quickly. Finding her voice, she yelled out, "Yes!"

Nick stood and kissed her passionately. They ignored the whoops from the small crowd that had assembled. Once they parted, he placed his hand around her waist and escorted her to his vehicle. He watched her as she looked lovingly up into his face.

"We've got parents to call and a party to show up at."

Morgan just nodded, she was speechless.

"Morgan?" he called her name. "Morgan, sweetheart, say something."

"I'm too stunned. Here I was ready to pour my heart out to you, to tell you how much I love you, and you go and lay this on me."

"I'm serious about the long engagement. We can wait a few years if you want to. But if you are pregnant, then we'll get married sooner."

She reached out and took his hand in hers, kissing the backs of it before holding it close to her heart. This was what she wanted. They slowed as they reached the SUV in the parking garage. He pulled her into his arms and placed his lips sweetly over hers. The moan escaped her throat as her hands snaked up his back and came to rest at the nape of his head. He broke the kiss.

"Thank you, Morgan. I know here." He tapped his chest. "That you love me. And I pray that no matter what, we will always love each other. And for the record, woman, I've been in love with you from the moment you sashayed your self into my bar and sat across from me."

Morgan pulled his face to hers, her mouth inviting, her body reacting to the feel of him—the passion in his kiss. There was no turning back.

"Morgan, we go forward. And if your father won't accept me, then we'll have to make him see that I won't become a drunk, not a big drinker, anyway. But if it gets too bad, then I'll just sell the bar to one of my brothers."

"You'd do that for me? I wouldn't let you do that. I'd be mad if you did."

He smiled, then rubbed her back as he kissed her again, this time lingering long, his lips, followed by his tongue ran smoothly across her lips, then trailed down her throat. "This is just the beginning, Morgan. Just the beginning."

Morgan showered and dressed quickly. She had been tired after her long flight from LA topped with knowing that tonight she and Nick would not only announce their dating, but their engagement. She thought of her father. She knew she had to get them together, get her father to see that Nick was the man she wanted to spend her life with.

A second wind caught up to her as Nick walked into her bedroom, dressed in a Olive suit, with a deep gold shirt and darker tie. "Wow, you clean up nicely, Mr. Chambers."

"Why, thank you. Ready?"

"I will be. Why don't you put on some music. I'll be finished in half an hour."

Nick disappeared. Moments later, the sounds of Anita Baker flowed through the speakers. The bass line introduced Body and Soul. The haunting words crept into Morgan. She reached out to Nick. He came in her arms, and they began to sway together. When the song hit its chorus, Morgan sang along. Her deep alto strained to match Anita's smoother one as she sung to Nick the words which told him exactly how she felt.

As the song ended, Nick stepped out of the bedroom. "I'll be right back."

Morgan completed her knit dress with a gold cartouche. She heard a knocking at her front door. She called out to Nick. When she got no reply, she walked out to the door.

"Who is it?" she asked.

"It's your blind date."

Morgan laughed and opened the door. "You're crazy. Get in here." She grabbed him by the hand and pulled him inside. She wrapped her arms around him, pulled him close, then smiled up at him as his eyes bore into her. She stood on the tips of her toes and kissed him lightly on the cheek. This was it. This was the beginning of always.

CHAPTER 17

Chicago's lakefront breezed by as Nick drove them along Lake Shore drive, heading to Jackson's house.

He held Morgan's hand as he maneuvered the SUV around the Sheridan Road curve. She laid her head on Nick's shoulder. As they pulled up in front of Jackson's house, Nick turned to face her.

"You ready?"

Morgan laughed. "I can't wait to see the look on Yavette's face. And you said Jackson hadn't told her we've gotten together?" She giggled. "This is gonna be great! As far as she knows, you just sent me flowers, and that's all."

"Nope, they don't even know that. I never told him that I actually sent them. He called me the other day to see if I wanted to go on with this charade."

"All right. I'll go in first, and then you follow minutes later."

Morgan jumped out of the car and headed up the walk. She rang the doorbell and waited. Jackson appeared at the door.

"Good to see you again, Morgan." He hugged her. She noticed he looked around behind her.

"Same here. How've you been?"

"No complaints." He held the door open and Morgan stepped across the threshold. She watched as he looked out behind her again before he shut the door.

Morgan stepped into the living room and greeted several cousins who had been chosen to be a part of the wedding. She moved further into the house and went in search of Yavette. Finding her in the kitchen, Morgan hugged her cousin, and then sat down at the center island. "Hey, girl, those shoes are bad." She pointed to the black, three-inch heels Yavette wore with a long black skirt and top.

"Well, you helped. What's up tonight? Ready to meet your third and final blind date?"

"I thought I asked you to skip it. Why are you trying to torture me? I thought I was your favorite cousin. No, you won't leave well enough alone. First I had to suffer through Mr. Thomas Almighty, then I had to deal with Tony Fake-a-nation! Now you want to hook me up with some dude who I don't even know and probably looks like—"

Morgan's act was interrupted by the sound of the doorbell. She looked at Yavette who'd seemed to shrink right before her eyes. "That better not be my 'blind date,'" Morgan said through clenched teeth as she looked toward the living room where she heard Nick's deep voice.

Jackson walked into the kitchen first, followed by Nick. Morgan wanted to laugh, the looks on both Yavette and Jackson's faces were unreal. They both looked as if they lost their best friends.

"Ummm, who's this lovely morsel?" Nick said as he walked over to Morgan and put his arm around her waist. She spied Jackson and Yavette give each other curious glances as Nick pulled Morgan to him and placed a loud kiss on her lips. "And tastes good, too!"

Nick and Morgan looked at Jackson and Yavette and began to laugh uncontrollably. Yavette stood next to Jackson with her mouth open as she looked from Morgan to Nick, and back to Morgan.

After several moments, Nick and Morgan sobered and explained what was going on.

"You mean to tell me that you two have been dating for the past two weeks?"

Morgan nodded her head to Yavette. "The night Tony stood me up, I went to the bar, and Nick and I went out. This is the man who used to fix my drinks every Friday night."

"But I thought you said his name was something else?" Yavette asked.

"I did. I told you his name was Jarrod. His name is Nicholas Jarrod Chambers, Jr." She went on to explain the name issue and how neither really knew the other until recently.

"And all this time you knew he was going to be your date for this party?"

"Yup." She she put her arm around Nick's waist. "Come on and let me introduce you to the clan. And let me warn you, this is just a fraction of the bunch."

For the rest of the evening, they sat and talked about the upcoming wedding for Jackson Fisher to Yavette Ramsey.

"That was a nice party, and smart of Yavette, too. Gave her a chance to see what we have to deal with over the next six months," Morgan said as they entered Nick's home. They had purposely decided to hold off announcing their engagement, even though it was hard for Morgan to hide the solitaire on her finger as she twisted the ring around to the inside of her palm.

She watched as Nick turned off the lights, then took her hand in his and led them upstairs. He sat down on the edge of the bed and placed his hand out to Morgan. She sat next to him and let the silence absorb them, their feelings around them. They remained quiet for several moments before Nick rose and turned on the miniature CD player next to his bed. Acoustics, which sounded like the soft blowing of the wind, signaled the Norman Connors' "You Are My Starship." Nick pulled Morgan from the bed and began to sing, his smooth voice sweet. She closed her eyes and felt him pull her closer, her back coming to rest against his shoulder, his mouth nestled near her hair.

As the song ended, it was quickly replaced with another—the Isley's "Sensuality." Morgan laughed slightly. She had never been serenaded before, and the richness of Nick's voice soothed her like a baby being lulled.

He wrapped his arm around her and pulled her close, their bodies touching, releasing the now all too familiar current between them. They began to sway slowly, her arms about his neck, her head on his wide chest. She listened to both the mellifluous song and the rapid beating of Nick's heart, the randy hardness in his pants.

"See, what you do to me," he whispered.

He gently took her face into his large hands and stared deeply at her. His face blurred as it came closer to hers. Her eyes became mere slits as she felt the smooth fullness of his lips meld with her own. She relished in the feeling, loved the way he nibbled and taunted, his hands now making their way down her back, stopping just above her full behind. When she thought she couldn't stand the play any longer, Nick's hand snaked up to her head, his fingers played, then plied her soft head of hair.

Their kiss intensified as they drank of each other. Shamelessly, Morgan let her hands roam across Nick's muscular back, down to his taut behind, then across the front of his well-formed thighs. She heard him moan.

His mouth recaptured hers, his tongue slowly darting in and out of her open mouth. Morgan felt herself swirling, falling into that vortex their lovemaking had created for them. Before she knew it, she was lying on top of Nick, feeling every hard inch of him.

This was it—the point of no return. Morgan began to slowly undulate her hips. She heard him moan, the sound rose deep from his chest. His hands had a mind of their own as they roamed, paused then ran up along the length of her body. He flipped Morgan over gently and removed her clothes. He bowed his head, placing it on her chest. He rested there, his nostrils flared as he inhaled the scent of her.

Nick undid the front clasp of her bra. He stared at her, shaking his head at the beauty of her, his woman. He began to nibble, suckle, nibble, suckle—each ministration elicited a moan from Morgan as she writhed beneath his torment. He played her like a finely tuned instrument, coaxing sounds from her, making her respond to his expertise. The louder Morgan moaned the more he suckled.

Morgan pleaded. "Baby, what have you done to me?"

"I want to make love to you every chance I get. I want to hear you call my name as I make you come. I want to feel your arms and legs wrapped around me. I want to feel your love, baby." He rubbed his hands down her now bare legs, pausing to stroke her folds.

"Please, Nick, make love me," she commanded, then pulled him closer, her hands on his smooth face, raining kisses all over his cheeks. "Now," she ordered as he rested his weight on his elbows and entered her with one full thrust. She began to shake involuntarily as her muscles tightened around him.

The heat, coupled with the tight wetness, was too much, and Nick's head begun to swim. He shook it slightly, in a vain attempt to regain his senses. Each time he moved, she moved, matching him. The release was there, threatening, calling. Morgan's hips crashed up to his. He released a guttural groan, pulling Morgan upward to sit on his lap. She moved slowly at first, twirling her hips then her movement became faster. Her own breathing came in short pants. Then he heard what he wanted to her. He heard her call out his name, her voice sweet.

"Nick," she sang over and again.

They were lost as their motions became one. In sync, their bodies moved toward the pinnacle. They were one: body, mind, and soul. As the release took over, they each called out to the other, holding on to the heated passion that made them drunk before it sedated them. As the passion took hold, Morgan called out her love for him.

"Spend the night," he breathed into her ear as he lowered their bodies to rest fully on the bed and wrapped her tightly in his arms.

CHAPTER 18

One month had passed, and Nick and Morgan continued to see each other, but her father had still refused to talk to Morgan. Yavette and Morgan had decided that Morgan should announce her engagement.

The day of the engagement party at Yavette's, she had called her father in hopes of at least getting him to agree to meet with Nick. Her father had turned her down, and she had no choice but to tell him where she stood.

"Daddy, Nick and I are engaged." She listened as he huffed right before hanging up the phone. Morgan squared her shoulders and tossed her head back. He had laid down the gauntlet, and she would stick with it.

Morgan held Nick's hand as they walked into the house that had become her second home while growing up.

"Morgan, come here girl," Aunt Etta said as she pulled Morgan into her arms, crushing her against her large bust. "How've you been? How's the business?"

"Good, Aunt Etta. How've you been?"

"A little pain in mah joints every now and then to remind me I'm no spring chicken. Other than that, I'm good." She looked up at Nick. "And let me guess, that's your beau?" Morgan nodded. "Come here, boy, and give me a hug. You're practically family now." Nick stepped into Aunt Etta's embrace and made a funny face at Morgan as he was crushed against her.

"Nice to meet you, too," Nick said as she released him.

Morgan took Nick's hand. "Aunt Etta, where's Uncle Bryce?"

"I think he's outside adding those heat lamps to the tent. But wait." Her aunt handed Morgan a dish. "Take this outside for me. Nick, you stay here."

Morgan looked suspiciously at her aunt, but took the dish from her and headed outside.

"Come. Let's talk in the den." Aunt Etta led Nick out of the kitchen. She sat down on a winged back chair and motioned for him to sit across from her.

"I hear my brother, Ishmael, is givin' y'all a hard time, but I'm not sure how much Morgan told you, and how much he's told her."

"She told me that Rev. Paige's father was an alcoholic."

"Is, baby, and will always be. My daddy gave up liquor thirty years ago when our mother got cancer. But before that, Daddy was a zip damn fool. He'd get paid on Friday, and would be broke by Saturday morning. He'd drink and gamble the money away. The more he gambled, the more he drank. The more he drank, the more he gambled. Ishmael is the second oldest, but the oldest male, and he took his role serious. Had it not been for Ishmael, we would have gone hungry a lot more than we did. And though he loves Daddy, we all agreed that he hasn't quite made the peace with Daddy he says he has. Your business just reminds him, that's all."

"I told Morgan that I'd sell it, but she said she'd be mad if I did."

"No need for all of that. You two are grown. Old enough to make your own choices, and your own decisions. If Ishmael wants to hold on to an attitude, I say let him." She waved her hand in the air. "Besides, Morgan's not getting any younger, and you two need to hurry up and get married and get started on some babies."

Nick chuckled at the order. He thought about Morgan getting her menses, yet they still had been foregoing using any protection.

"Well, that's all I wanted to say, and welcome to the family."

"Thank you, Mrs. Ramsey."

"Baby, call me Aunt Etta."

"Okay, Aunt Etta," he said, then rose and placed a kiss on her cheek. "Thanks a lot."

Nick found Morgan in the heated tent set up in the backyard. She looked up as he entered the tent. She turned when she heard her name called, and to see Mr. Chambers coming toward her. He opened his arms and embraced her.

"Hi, there, daughter. How are you today?"

"I'm okay, Mr. Chambers."

He slapped his son on the shoulder, then turned his attention back to Morgan. "Call me Papa. I'd like that." He placed a pliant kiss on Morgan's cheek.

Nick's father went over to Jackson and shook his hand. He looked at Yavette and pulled her into a bear hug. Morgan and Nick laughed at the surprised expression on her face.

Within an hour, everyone was present and standing under the large tent. Morgan's parents had arrived, and were standing off to the side, speaking with various family members present. Morgan watched her father dismiss her as he went from one of his siblings to another. She noticed that each sibling he tried to speak to waved a hand at him. He looked shunned.

Everyone's attention was grabbed by Jackson, whose voice sounded over the microphone hooked up to the DJ's equipment.

"Yavette and I would like to thank you for coming out tonight and sharing this special day with us. This is just the beginning. We've set a date, and we hope to see each and every one of you on April fourth as we make this union permanent."

Everyone clapped.

"Tonight we're going to do something a little un-orthodox. It's not everyday that a man finds the woman he wants to spend the rest of his life with, commit to share all the ups and down life has to offer. With Yavette, I've found this. So, with this said, I'm pleased to turn this whole affair over to a man who's like my brother, my best friend and best man."

A smiling Nick stepped forward and accepted the microphone from Jackson's hand. His eyes never left Morgan's. He looked out over the crowd assembled and took comfort in seeing his father, his brothers, Nehemiah and David, and David's wife, Alexis. He also saw Tina as she stood close to Nehemiah.

"Jackson is right." He walked over to Morgan and took her hand in his. "To find someone to share your life in this crazy mixed up world is important. For me, I've found her." He kissed her hand. "This beautiful lady has agreed to become my wife. Now, Mr. Paige, I know you don't agree with my line of work, and when I mentioned to Morgan that I would sell the bar versus allowing it to come between you two, she refused to entertain that thought. Sir, I won't be selling my business. It's been in the family for almost four decades. And if Morgan and I are blessed to have children, I will pass my businesses, including the bar, to them. But I am asking you to reconsider and give Morgan and I your blessing."

All heads turned to look at Morgan's father. He looked at the eyes staring at him, and the man who stood before him holding the hand of his only child. His eyes went from Morgan to Nick, and he could see that, though they were asking for his blessing, it was evident that they'd marry without it.

Those in attendance seemed to hold their breath as Ishmael came forward and extended his hand to Nick. He pulled Nick into an embrace and whispered, "You may marry my daughter. Just take care of her, and don't hurt her."

"Never," Nick whispered back.

Cheers went up as the two men embraced again before Ishmael reached out to Morgan.

EPILOGUE

"Sit still, Morgan," Yavette ordered as she adjusted the straps to Morgan's wedding gown, a tea-length, fitted satin dress adorned with mother of pearl from the bodice to the end.

"Girl, you're gonna make me stick you if you don't sit still."

Morgan looked into the mirror at her cousin. She leaned back enough to reach out and fill her cousin's protruding stomach. Yavette was due any day, and Morgan was surprised that her cousin had actually made the wedding. Morgan had chosen her mother to act as her maid of honor.

As the music began, Morgan rose from the seat and looked at her reflection in the mirror. For over a year, she and Nick reveled in their love as they learned more and more about the other. And just as she had said, her father did like Nick, to the point that they now spent hours discussing any and all of the latest topics in the news.

She stepped out of the rear of the vestibule and met Nick's father at the rear of the small chapel. She took his offered arm and began walking down the aisle. Tears streamed down her face as she neared the alter—her intended husband to the right, and her father beaming proudly from the center.

Nick stepped down to meet her, and her soon to be father-in-law kissed her on the cheek, hugged his middle child and stepped back. Morgan smiled at her father as he began the marriage ceremony.

Finally, she thought as she looked up into Nick's intense light eyes, *no more blind dates. Nick is the hero I was holding out for. Thank God. I could have gotten stuck with Lawrence.*

ABOUT THE AUTHOR

Cupid is the sixth title by **Barbara Keaton**, who lives in Chicago and works for the Chicago Transit Authority. An admitted romantic at heart, Barbara credits her love of the written word to her late Grandfather, Thomas Hill, and to the Oblate Sisters of Providence, one of the oldest known orders of Black Nuns in the world.

CUPID

2006 Publication Schedule

2006 Publication Schedule (continued)

July

Love Me Carefully
A.C. Arthur
1-58571-177-2
$9.95

No Ordinary Love
Angela Weaver
1-58571-198-5
$9.95

Rehoboth Road
Anita Ballard-Jones
1-58571-196-9
$12.95

August

Scent of Rain
Annetta P. Lee
158571-199-3
$9.95

Love in High Gear
Charlotte Roy
158571-185-3
$9.95

Rise of the Phoenix
Kenneth Whetstone
1-58571-197-7
$12.95

September

The Business of Love
Cheris Hodges
1-58571-193-4
$9.95

Rock Star
Rosyln Hardy Holcomb
1-58571-200-0
$9.95

A Dead Man Speaks
Lisa Jones Johnson
1-58571-203-5
$12.95

October

Rivers of the Soul-Part 1
Leslie Esdaile
1-58571-223-X
$9.95

A Dangerous Woman
J.M. Jeffries
1-58571-195-0
$9.95

Sinful Intentions
Crystal Rhodes
1-58571-201-9
$12.95

November

Only You
Crystal Hubbard
1-58571-208-6
$9.95

Ebony Eyes
Kei Swanson
1-58571-194-2
$9.95

Still Waters Run Deep –
Part 2
Leslie Esdaile
1-58571-224-8
$9.95

December

Let's Get It On
Dyanne Davis
1-58571-210-8
$9.95

Nights Over Egypt
Barbara Keaton
1-58571-192-6
$9.95

A Perfect Place to Pray
I.L. Goodwin
1-58571-202-7
$12.95

Other Genesis Press, Inc. Titles

A Dangerous Deception	J.M. Jeffries	$8.95
A Dangerous Love	J.M. Jeffries	$8.95
A Dangerous Obsession	J.M. Jeffries	$8.95
A Drummer's Beat to Mend	Kei Swanson	$9.95
A Happy Life	Charlotte Harris	$9.95
A Heart's Awakening	Veronica Parker	$9.95
A Lark on the Wing	Phyliss Hamilton	$9.95
A Love of Her Own	Cheris F. Hodges	$9.95
'A Love to Cherish	Beverly Clark	$8.95
A Risk of Rain	Dar Tomlinson	$8.95
A Twist of Fate	Beverly Clark	$8.95
A Will to Love	Angie Daniels	$9.95
Acquisitions	Kimberley White	$8.95
Across	Carol Payne	$12.95
After the Vows	Leslie Esdaile	$10.95
(Summer Anthology)	T.T. Henderson	
	Jacqueline Thomas	
Again My Love	Kayla Perrin	$10.95
Against the Wind	Gwynne Forster	$8.95
All I Ask	Barbara Keaton	$8.95
Ambrosia	T.T. Henderson	$8.95
An Unfinished Love Affair	Barbara Keaton	$8.95
And Then Came You	Dorothy Elizabeth Love	$8.95
Angel's Paradise	Janice Angelique	$9.95
At Last	Lisa G. Riley	$8.95
Best of Friends	Natalie Dunbar	$8.95
Beyond the Rapture	Beverly Clark	$9.95
Blaze	Barbara Keaton	$9.95
Blood Lust	J. M. Jeffries	$9.95
Bodyguard	Andrea Jackson	$9.95
Boss of Me	Diana Nyad	$8.95
Bound by Love	Beverly Clark	$8.95
Breeze	Robin Hampton Allen	$10.95

Other Genesis Press, Inc. Titles (continued)

Broken	Dar Tomlinson	$24.95
By Design	Barbara Keaton	$8.95
Cajun Heat	Charlene Berry	$8.95
Careless Whispers	Rochelle Alers	$8.95
Cats & Other Tales	Marilyn Wagner	$8.95
Caught in a Trap	Andre Michelle	$8.95
Caught Up In the Rapture	Lisa G. Riley	$9.95
Cautious Heart	Cheris F Hodges	$8.95
Chances	Pamela Leigh Starr	$8.95
Cherish the Flame	Beverly Clark	$8.95
Class Reunion	Irma Jenkins/John Brown	$12.95
Code Name: Diva	J.M. Jeffries	$9.95
Conquering Dr. Wexler's Heart	Kimberley White	$9.95
Crossing Paths, Tempting Memories	Dorothy Elizabeth Love	$9.95
Cypress Whisperings	Phyllis Hamilton	$8.95
Dark Embrace	Crystal Wilson Harris	$8.95
Dark Storm Rising	Chinelu Moore	$10.95
Daughter of the Wind	Joan Xian	$8.95
Deadly Sacrifice	Jack Kean	$22.95
Designer Passion	Dar Tomlinson	$8.95
Dreamtective	Liz Swados	$5.95
Ebony Butterfly II	Delilah Dawson	$14.95
Echoes of Yesterday	Beverly Clark	$9.95
Eden's Garden	Elizabeth Rose	$8.95
Everlastin' Love	Gay G. Gunn	$8.95
Everlasting Moments	Dorothy Elizabeth Love	$8.95
Everything and More	Sinclair Lebeau	$8.95
Everything but Love	Natalie Dunbar	$8.95
Eve's Prescription	Edwina Martin Arnold	$8.95
Falling	Natalie Dunbar	$9.95
Fate	Pamela Leigh Starr	$8.95
Finding Isabella	A.J. Garrotto	$8.95

Other Genesis Press, Inc. Titles (continued)

Forbidden Quest	Dar Tomlinson	$10.95
Forever Love	Wanda Thomas	$8.95
From the Ashes	Kathleen Suzanne	$8.95
	Jeanne Sumerix	
Gentle Yearning	Rochelle Alers	$10.95
Glory of Love	Sinclair LeBeau	$10.95
Go Gentle into that Good Night	Malcom Boyd	$12.95
Goldengroove	Mary Beth Craft	$16.95
Groove, Bang, and Jive	Steve Cannon	$8.99
Hand in Glove	Andrea Jackson	$9.95
Hard to Love	Kimberley White	$9.95
Hart & Soul	Angie Daniels	$8.95
Heartbeat	Stephanie Bedwell-Grime	$8.95
Hearts Remember	M. Loui Quezada	$8.95
Hidden Memories	Robin Allen	$10.95
Higher Ground	Leah Latimer	$19.95
Hitler, the War, and the Pope	Ronald Rychiak	$26.95
How to Write a Romance	Kathryn Falk	$18.95
I Married a Reclining Chair	Lisa M. Fuhs	$8.95
Indigo After Dark Vol. I	Nia Dixon/Angelique	$10.95
Indigo After Dark Vol. II	Dolores Bundy/Cole Riley	$10.95
Indigo After Dark Vol. III	Montana Blue/Coco Morena	$10.95
Indigo After Dark Vol. IV	Cassandra Colt/	$14.95
	Diana Richeaux	
Indigo After Dark Vol. V	Delilah Dawson	$14.95
Icie	Pamela Leigh Starr	$8.95
I'll Be Your Shelter	Giselle Carmichael	$8.95
I'll Paint a Sun	A.J. Garrotto	$9.95
Illusions	Pamela Leigh Starr	$8.95
Indiscretions	Donna Hill	$8.95
Intentional Mistakes	Michele Sudler	$9.95
Interlude	Donna Hill	$8.95
Intimate Intentions	Angie Daniels	$8.95

Other Genesis Press, Inc. Titles (continued)

Other Genesis Press, Inc. Titles (continued)

Object of His Desire	A. C. Arthur	$8.95
Office Policy	A. C. Arthur	$9.95
Once in a Blue Moon	Dorianne Cole	$9.95
One Day at a Time	Bella McFarland	$8.95
Outside Chance	Louisa Dixon	$24.95
Passion	T.T. Henderson	$10.95
Passion's Blood	Cherif Fortin	$22.95
Passion's Journey	Wanda Thomas	$8.95
Past Promises	Jahmel West	$8.95
Path of Fire	T.T. Henderson	$8.95
Path of Thorns	Annetta P. Lee	$9.95
Peace Be Still	Colette Haywood	$12.95
Picture Perfect	Reon Carter	$8.95
Playing for Keeps	Stephanie Salinas	$8.95
Pride & Joi	Gay G. Gunn	$15.95
Pride & Joi	Gay G. Gunn	$8.95
Promises to Keep	Alicia Wiggins	$8.95
Quiet Storm	Donna Hill	$10.95
Reckless Surrender	Rochelle Alers	$6.95
Red Polka Dot in a World of Plaid	Varian Johnson	$12.95
Reluctant Captive	Joyce Jackson	$8.95
Rendezvous with Fate	Jeanne Sumerix	$8.95
Revelations	Cheris F. Hodges	$8.95
Rivers of the Soul	Leslie Esdaile	$8.95
Rocky Mountain Romance	Kathleen Suzanne	$8.95
Rooms of the Heart	Donna Hill	$8.95
Rough on Rats and Tough on Cats	Chris Parker	$12.95
Secret Library Vol. 1	Nina Sheridan	$18.95
Secret Library Vol. 2	Cassandra Colt	$8.95
Shades of Brown	Denise Becker	$8.95
Shades of Desire	Monica White	$8.95

Other Genesis Press, Inc. Titles (continued)

Shadows in the Moonlight	Jeanne Sumerix	$8.95
Sin	Crystal Rhodes	$8.95
So Amazing	Sinclair LeBeau	$8.95
Somebody's Someone	Sinclair LeBeau	$8.95
Someone to Love	Alicia Wiggins	$8.95
Song in the Park	Martin Brant	$15.95
Soul Eyes	Wayne L. Wilson	$12.95
Soul to Soul	Donna Hill	$8.95
Southern Comfort	J.M. Jeffries	$8.95
Still the Storm	Sharon Robinson	$8.95
Still Waters Run Deep	Leslie Esdaile	$8.95
Stories to Excite You	Anna Forrest/Divine	$14.95
Subtle Secrets	Wanda Y. Thomas	$8.95
Suddenly You	Crystal Hubbard	$9.95
Sweet Repercussions	Kimberley White	$9.95
Sweet Tomorrows	Kimberly White	$8.95
Taken by You	Dorothy Elizabeth Love	$9.95
Tattooed Tears	T. T. Henderson	$8.95
The Color Line	Lizzette Grayson Carter	$9.95
The Color of Trouble	Dyanne Davis	$8.95
The Disappearance of Allison Jones	Kayla Perrin	$5.95
The Honey Dipper's Legacy	Pannell-Allen	$14.95
The Joker's Love Tune	Sidney Rickman	$15.95
The Little Pretender	Barbara Cartland	$10.95
The Love We Had	Natalie Dunbar	$8.95
The Man Who Could Fly	Bob & Milana Beamon	$18.95
The Missing Link	Charlyne Dickerson	$8.95
The Price of Love	Sinclair LeBeau	$8.95
The Smoking Life	Ilene Barth	$29.95
The Words of the Pitcher	Kei Swanson	$8.95
Three Wishes	Seressia Glass	$8.95
Ties That Bind	Kathleen Suzanne	$8.95
Tiger Woods	Libby Hughes	$5.95

Other Genesis Press, Inc. Titles (continued)

Time is of the Essence	Angie Daniels	$9.95
Timeless Devotion	Bella McFarland	$9.95
Tomorrow's Promise	Leslie Esdaile	$8.95
Truly Inseparable	Wanda Y. Thomas	$8.95
Unbreak My Heart	Dar Tomlinson	$8.95
Uncommon Prayer	Kenneth Swanson	$9.95
Unconditional	A.C. Arthur	$9.95
Unconditional Love	Alicia Wiggins	$8.95
Until Death Do Us Part	Susan Paul	$8.95
Vows of Passion	Bella McFarland	$9.95
Wedding Gown	Dyanne Davis	$8.95
What's Under Benjamin's Bed	Sandra Schaffer	$8.95
When Dreams Float	Dorothy Elizabeth Love	$8.95
Whispers in the Night	Dorothy Elizabeth Love	$8.95
Whispers in the Sand	LaFlorya Gauthier	$10.95
Wild Ravens	Altonya Washington	$9.95
Yesterday Is Gone	Beverly Clark	$10.95
Yesterday's Dreams, Tomorrow's Promises	Reon Laudat	$8.95
Your Precious Love	Sinclair LeBeau	$8.95

Order Form

Mail to: Genesis Press, Inc.
P.O. Box 101
Columbus, MS 39703

Name _____
Address _____
City/State _____ Zip _____
Telephone _____

Ship to (if different from above)
Name _____
Address _____
City/State _____ Zip _____
Telephone _____

Credit Card Information
Credit Card # _____ ☐ Visa   ☐ Mastercard
Expiration Date (mm/yy) _____ ☐ AmEx ☐ Discover

Qty.	Author	Title	Price	Total

Use this order

form, or call

1-888-INDIGO-1

Total for books	_____
Shipping and handling:	
$5 first two books,	
$1 each additional book	_____
Total S & H	_____
Total amount enclosed	_____

Mississippi residents add 7% sales tax